DANCING

ARABS

SAYED KASHUA

Translated from the Hebrew
by
Miriam Shlesinger

D1053908

Grove Press
New York

Copyright © 2002 by Sayed Kashua
Translation copyright © 2004 by Miriam Shlesinger

All rights reserved. No part of this book may be reproduced in any form or by any
electronic or mechanical means, including information storage and retrieval systems,
without permission in writing from the publisher, except by a reviewer, who may
quote brief passages in a review. Any members of educational institutions wishing to
photocopy part or all of the work for classroom use, or publishers who would like to
obtain permission to include the work in an anthology, should send their inquiries to
Grove/Atlantic, Inc., 841 Broadway, New York, NY 10003.

First published in the Hebrew language by Modan Publishing House, Ltd.

Published simultaneously in Canada
Printed in the United States of America

FIRST EDITION

Library of Congress Cataloging-in-Publication Data
Qashu, Sayed, 1975–
['Arvim rokdim. English]
Dancing Arabs / by Sayed Kashua ; translated from the Hebrew by Miriam Shlesinger.
p. cm.
ISBN 0-8021-4126-9
I. Children, Palestinian Arab—Fiction.   I. Shlesinger, Miriam, 1947–   II. Title.
PJ5055.38.A84A8713 2004
892.4'37—dc22   2003067765

Grove Press
841 Broadway
New York, NY 10003

04 05 06 07   10 9 8 7 6 5 4 3 2 1

International Praise for *Dancing Arabs:*

"A beautiful and moving novel . . . The great innovation in Sayed Kashua's book is the sense that every line is the whole truth and nothing but the truth." —*Ha'aretz* (Israel)

"An astonishing book . . . without self-righteousness [Kashua] illuminates the hell of anguished cohabitation and the prejudices that foment fear." —*La Liberte* (France)

"Mixing slapstick and desperation, war and daily life, grand political scenarios and individual tragedy . . . *Dancing Arabs* captures the double bind of Arab-Israelis."
—*Panorama* (Italy)

"*Dancing Arabs* is a delight despite its bitter truth. Kashua and his anti-hero laugh, and in that is more heroism than in any explosive belt." —*Neue Zuricher Zeitung* (Switzerland)

"[Kashua's] hero does not have a God. He does not threaten with violence, nor does he ask for pity. . . . His life is a masquerade ball, and though he betrays himself, disguises himself, and pours himself from one character to another, he is always honest. And no reader, foreign or local, can remain indifferent to his truth."
—Dorit Rabinyan, author of *Persian Brides*

"Anyone who wants to understand what is happening to the Arab society in Israel has to read this excellent first novel. . . . It is difficult to imagine an empathy greater than the one displayed by this writer towards his family, his childhood landscape and his people."   —*Ma'ariv* (Israel)

"A striking satire."   —*Die Welt* (Germany)

DANCING
ARABS

DANCING
ARABS

PART ONE

Grandma's Death Equipment

The Keys
to the Cupboard

I was always looking for the keys to the cupboard. I looked for them every time Grandma went to visit the home of another old woman in the village who had died. The old brown cupboard was like a locked trunk with a treasure inside—diamonds and royal jewels. One morning, after another night when I'd sneaked into her bed because I was too scared to fall asleep, I saw her take the key out of a hidden pocket she'd sewn in one of her pillows. Grandma handed me the key and asked me to take her prayer rug out of the cupboard for her. I leaped out of bed at once. What had come over her? Was she really letting me open the cupboard? I took the key, and as soon as I put it in the lock, Grandma said, "Turn it gently. Everything is rusty by now."

White dresses were hanging in one section, and in the other were shelves with towels, folded *sharwals*, and stockings. No underpants. Grandma didn't wear underwear, just *sharwals*. The sheepskin prayer rug was on the bottom shelf. She'd made it herself: bought the sheep on 'id el-fitr, skinned it, salted it, and dried it in the sun. On the top shelf she'd put an enormous blue suitcase, the one she'd taken on her hajj a few years earlier.

What's she got in there? I wondered. Maybe a few more of those policemen's outfits, like the ones she brought back to us from Mecca.

I pulled the rug off the shelf and spread it out on the spot where Grandma always said her prayers. She would pray sitting down, because by then it was hard for her to kneel for so long.

Grandma lives with us. Actually, we live with her. She has her own room, with her own bathroom and a basin for washing her hands before saying her prayers, and she never passes through the living room or the kitchen. The way she sees it, anyone who wants her has to go into her room. She would never dream of invading Mother's territory. And if my parents would rather not talk to her, that's fine too; she has no intention of striking up a conversation. It used to be her house once, until my father, her only son, took it over, added a few rooms, got married, and had kids of his own. Of Grandma's four grandsons, I was the only one who would crawl into bed with her. I almost never slept in the room I shared with my brothers. I'd always wait for my parents to fall asleep, and then, very very quietly, I'd sneak into Grandma's room, into her bed. She knew I was afraid—of thieves, of the dark, of monsters. She knew that with her I felt protected, and she never told me not to come, never said, Don't crawl into bed with me anymore, even though it was a twin bed and more than thirty years old. Every morning I'd wake at dawn, when Grandma would be saying her prayers. I'd never seen the key. She'd never asked me to bring her anything from the cupboard.

When she finished praying that morning, she turned to me. "Did you see where I hide the key? You're the only one I'm telling, and I want you to promise me not to tell anyone else till the day I die. Then you'll open the cupboard and tell your aunts—they're bound to come here when I'm dead—that all the equipment is in the blue bag. You understand? They mustn't use anything except that equipment. Promise?"

I promised.

"And it's time you stopped being afraid. Such a smart boy, what are you afraid of? Hurry up, off to your room before your parents wake up."

Now I'm the one in charge of Grandma's death. She must know something I don't. Otherwise, what would she need death equipment for? And what is death equipment anyway?

After that morning when Grandma told me where the key was hidden, I started racing home every recess. I only had five minutes, but we lived really close to the school. When the bell rang, I could hear it from our house, and I always made it back to class before the teacher had covered the distance from the teachers' room. I was never late. I was the best student in the class, the best in the whole fourth grade. Every time I ran home, I imagined my grandmother lying in her twin bed with her four daughters standing over her, weeping and singing the very same songs they sang when Uncle Bashir, Aunt Fahten's husband, died or when Uncle Shakker, Aunt Ibtissam's husband, died. I knew I mustn't miss Grandma's death, and I always prayed that

I'd make it back before they buried her. I had to get there in time to tell them about the blue suitcase. I had to tell them about the death equipment. Nobody knew where the key was, not even my father, her only male offspring.

At night, I continued sneaking off to Grandma's bed and sleeping beside her. But instead of being afraid of the dark, of thieves, and of dogs, I started being afraid that the woman next to me would die. Her large body no longer gave me a feeling of security. From that point on, I started sleeping with her to protect her. I would wake up very often, holding my breath and putting the back of my hand to her mouth. So long as I could feel the warm air, I knew—Not yet; death hasn't come yet.

Grandma didn't mention the blue bag of death equipment again, as if she'd forgotten all about it, as if her death wasn't on her mind anymore. Then, at some point in fifth grade, between winter break and spring break, when I dashed home during recess as usual, Grandma wasn't there. Grandma rarely left her room unless someone had died. And when she did, it took her a long time to return.

Without thinking twice I walked over to the pillow. Gently, without moving it, I pushed my hand into the secret pocket and pulled out the key. I remembered Grandma saying that everything was rusty, so I turned the key slowly and carefully. That's all I needed—for it to break off in the lock.

The things in the cupboard were just as they had been, as if nothing had changed: the rug, the white dresses, the *sharwals*. No underpants, only stockings. I couldn't reach the top shelf.

I took off my shoes, placed one foot on the shelf with the rug and the other one on the *sharwal* shelf, and managed to open the metal locks of the blue suitcase with one hand.

I could hardly see what it held, but I could feel towels. What, only towels? Is that the death equipment: towels? But the whole house is full of towels. Since when are there special death towels?

I ran to the kitchen to get a chair and stood on it. Just then I heard the bell. Another lesson was starting, but I was not going to run straight back this time. Let them mark me absent. I'd say I had a stomachache. They'd believe me because I'm a good student. I forgot about the bell and focused on the suitcase. Up on the chair I could reach it much more easily. I mustered all my strength before lifting it, but the suitcase was much lighter than I'd imagined. For some reason, I'd expected the death equipment to be heavy.

I put the suitcase down on Grandma's bed and studied its contents. The towels on top were meticulously folded. I took them out, one by one, making a mental note of the position of each one so I could replace it exactly. There were five of them. Underneath was a large piece of white fabric with the word *Mecca* written on it. My grandma must want them to use this cloth for her shroud. Underneath, there were dozens of bars of soap, all made in Mecca. There were perfume and hand cream too, a pair of tweezers still in its wrapping, scissors, and a new hairbrush. I didn't know that the death equipment was toiletries. I was very disappointed. Is this what I was missing agriculture class for—soaps and towels?

Now that all the equipment was out of the suitcase, I saw it was lined with newspapers. I was sure they were just there to protect the equipment from humidity, but before I had a chance to put the toiletries back inside, my eyes fell on a picture in one of the papers. It was all written in Hebrew, and I hadn't learned Hebrew well enough yet to read a paper, but in the newsprint I saw a small faded passport photo of a young man looking at me.

My hands froze. It was a picture of my father. True, he looked much younger. I'd never seen a picture of him at that age, but I could swear it was my father.

I lifted the paper, and underneath it were many more newspapers using that old passport photo. All of them were in Hebrew, and in class we were still plodding through "Who is this? This is Father. Who is this? This is Mother." I made up my mind: *I've got to learn Hebrew. I've got to be able to read a Hebrew newspaper.*

I rummaged some more and found dozens of postcards hidden underneath. These were in Arabic. I recognized my father's handwriting right away: beautiful and rounded, like a drawing. My father had been the best student in Tira. I'd always wanted to be like him.

I pulled out a postcard and read:

Dear Bashir,

How is my sister Fahten? I hope everything is well with you. I am fine, thank goodness. Tell Mother to stop crying. I will be released soon. Give my love to Sharifa, Fahten, Ibtissam, Shuruk, and the children.

P.S. There are a few things I would like Mother to bring on her next visit: a notebook, two pencils, a pair of socks, and two pair of underpants.

Yours,

Your brother Darwish

There were many red triangles on the postcard, with some Hebrew writing inside them, and on the back was a black-and-white picture of a girl soldier eating a falafel. Another bell went off. They were breaking for recess, and class would be starting again soon.

I quickly arranged the postcards and the papers the way they were before, put all the equipment back in the suitcase, and placed the suitcase back on the top shelf. After locking the cupboard, I pushed the key into the hidden pocket, and within two minutes I had returned the chair to the kitchen, put my shoes on, locked the front door, and was running back to class.

On my way, I saw a funeral. I spotted my grandmother. It was Abu Ziad who had died, our neighbor, whose grandson Ibrahim was in my class. My grandmother couldn't stand the sight of Abu Ziad. As for me, I couldn't stand the sight of Ibrahim.

The Best-looking,
the Smartest

One day when my father was a young man, he was sitting on the bed and listening to the radio.

"I don't know what he was listening to," Grandma says, "but all of a sudden he gave out a *Yes!* and jumped to the ceiling. Where did he take the strength from? He literally flew through the air. It gave me a fright, and I said, 'In the name of Allah the Merciful, what happened to you, *yamma*?'"

My father didn't answer. Grandma says he had a smile on his face, the likes of which she'd never seen before, and he packed a bag at once, kissed her, and said he was returning to Jerusalem.

A few hours later, the A-Daula—the State—arrived at our door. There must have been a hundred soldiers and policemen. Grandma was alone in the house. My four aunts were married already. "They searched every corner of the house. They had instruments that beeped, and they ran them over every stone. They turned the cupboards upside down, and the beds too. I said to them, 'Tell me what you're looking for, and maybe I can help you,' but they didn't answer. They went through every page in your father's books, took some of them, and left others behind. They went through his papers too. Then they started on the garden, digging up every inch." They'd been searching for weapons, of course, but she didn't figure that out until after they'd left. "I knew something had happened to him. I begged them to tell me if my son was all right, to tell me what had happened, but they didn't answer."

Grandma says my father never gave her so much as a single moment of peace. Ever. Grandma loves him very much. She says she loves him more than she loves herself. She was so keen for him to study at the university, she did everything she could to get him the tuition, the rent, and the spending money. She worked like two men, and everything she earned was for him. He lacked for nothing. Nobody would have guessed he was fatherless. He was the cleanest child in the class, the best-looking in the school. His clothes were always neat and ironed.

My grandma says he would go to school like a prince. Everyone envied him. Lots of kids beat up on him, and Grandma would head straight for their homes and shout at them and their parents. Anyone who tried to pull anything with my father knew he'd have my grandma to answer to. He was the best student. He studied a lot. Every night he'd sit up and study by candlelight, and when our neighbor would start singing—she loved to do that right in the middle of the night—he would light the kerosene heater so the noise would drown out her voice. He paced the fields with his books in hand and got the highest grades.

On graduation day my Uncle Bashir, *Allah yerakhamu*, waited for him at the gate, and as soon as the ceremony was over he lifted my father up high, seated him on his shoulders, and danced all the way home. Uncle Bashir was a hero. He was broad as a camel. Barely made it through the door.

You couldn't tell that my father had no brothers and no father to take care of him. Even when she had no money for food, Grandma would buy him any book he asked for. She also bought him an expensive bike. She didn't want anyone thinking she was poor. She'd always tell me how she used to stuff plastic bags into the quilts, so her neighbors would think there was money rustling inside. No one could figure out how a widow who worked as a fruit picker could have money, but she just always said, God provides.

And then everything came tumbling down around her: her son, her investment, his studies. Even Grandma didn't know where he was. They said he was with the army. She couldn't sleep till she saw him. Uncle Bashir and Uncle Shakker—Aunt Ibtissam's husband—helped her comb every prison in the country. They didn't have a car, so they had to take buses. First they were told he was in Maskubieh, then in Ramla, then in Shatta, in Damon, in Beersheba.

Only two weeks later did she see him being taken to the detention center. She says she cried and screamed. He seemed smaller than usual, and he looked hungry. She always used the same words to describe what had happened there, and she'd always hold her white handkerchief in her hand, lifting it and lowering it at a mourner's pace, as if she'd filled it with sand and was pouring the sand over her head. "They're killing you, *yamma*. Did they beat you? What have they done to you, *yamma, ya habibi*?"

Grandma says that was just the beginning. She didn't have money for bus fare, so she started borrowing from my aunts to make the weekly trip, every Friday. She didn't miss a single visit, and she went for every remand. She didn't understand what they were saying. She just wanted to see him again, to know he was all right. She would never forgive herself if she missed even a single opportunity to see him. And she never went empty-handed. Always took him something to eat or something to wear, so he wouldn't get the idea that she was lacking for anything.

Her legs grew weaker. Her joints turned to soap, and she began using a cane. My father had been remanded yet again, without any evidence being produced. It was the Shabak, the General Security Service, that had demanded those remands, and the material was classified. All they said was "Dangerous, dangerous." It's known as administrative detention. They took him to a different detention center each time and never bothered to let Grandma know. She would have to go to great lengths to find out he'd been transferred, for example, from Shatta prison to Damon prison.

She learned the ropes in no time. She developed ties with Arab members of the Knesset, the ones people referred to as Druze dignitaries and Arab dignitaries. She wrote to all the newspapers. Every week she'd send out letters to all of them, written for her by people in the village who had a nice handwriting. She dictated: *Give me my son back. I have nothing in the world except him. You're killing me.* Sometimes one of her letters appeared in print. She kept all of them in the blue suitcase. She'd go to different villages in the Galilee and meet with anyone she thought could help: mayors, mukhtars, Druze clergymen. Time and time again, she'd visit them. She'd make them write letters to judges, to the police, to the government. "All he did was go to study," she'd explain to them. "They're just jealous. Those goddamn bastards informed on him, because he's the best-looking, the smartest."

My father wasn't scared. He knew Gamal Abdel Nasser would get him out. And he didn't get worked up about the way they treated him in the interrogations—the beatings and all. Sometimes later, when he watched television, he'd recognize one of the guys who questioned him. There were lots of well-known people about whom he could say, "That guy hit me once." To this day, he still rubs his hand up and down his cheek as he says it.

Father did everything he could to get out of jail. Once he cried for hours to convince the wardens that he had a toothache, just so they'd take him to the hospital. Father says the sonofabitch dentist knew there was nothing wrong with him but pulled one of his teeth anyway, without an anesthetic. "It was worth it just to get out for a while," he always says.

In the album there's one picture of my father sitting with someone on a high balcony. They're wearing heavy jackets and their hands are buried inside. They're freezing, struggling hard to warm up. Father says they sat on that balcony on the day of the Battle of Karama and counted the helicopters transferring wounded soldiers from Jordan to Hadassah hospital, he and his friend Halil from Tur'an. They were both detained for the same incident, but he didn't tell us what it was. It said in the papers that they'd bombed the university cafeteria, but Father says the papers always lie. Fact is, the day he was released, he bought a copy of *Ha'aretz* and it said that, according to Moshe Dayan, the student they'd detained posed a tangible threat to state security and was not going to be released in the foreseeable future. My father was released pretty quickly. It took Halil seventeen years. He was given a life sentence, but the Ahmad Jibril prisoner exchange saved him.

A few days after Halil was released, Father loaded the four of us in the backseat, and we set out on the long trip north to Tur'an, Halil's village. Father asked people where Halil lived. Some of them said they didn't know, because there was this crazy "rabbi" of theirs, Kahana, who promised to make sure the released prisoners were sent back to jail, so people were afraid to talk. People in Tur'an had a strange accent, and all of us laughed at them behind their backs because they stressed their *k*s. Father and Halil exchanged long hugs and kisses. I'd never seen such kissing. Halil didn't know we'd be coming, and his mother was pretty frightened to see us there all of a sudden. But then they said we were all one family, that Halil and my father were like brothers, and they invited us to stay the night. Halil and his whole family had that strange Tur'an accent too. We could hardly make out what they were saying.

While we were there, Father said that he and Halil and one other student from Jaljulya had once rented a house in Jerusalem from Rehavam Ze'evi's mother. Ze'evi was commanding officer of Central Command at the time. He was well-known for his right-wing philosophy, and everyone called him by his nickname, Gandhi. When his mother opened the door she said, "I'm Gandhi's mother. You must have heard of him?" and the guy from Jaljulya answered, "Sure, Gandhi the Indian," and the two of them—Father and Halil—couldn't stop laughing. Gandhi was married by then, and my father got his room. He says the library in that room was really something; he took a few books of revisionist philosophy by Jabotinsky. There were lots of war books too. His mother was nice and only asked them to make sure the neighbors didn't find out they were Arabs. My father says she must be dead by now. She was very old even then, and used to volunteer at Shaarei Tsedek hospital every day, cutting gauze.

After the Six-Day War they left Gandhi's mother's house, and when the army opened the way into the Old City, Father and Halil were among the first to go visit the Dome of the Rock. Father says they were very disappointed, because they'd been expecting to see a holy rock suspended over the mosque. Later, my father became a Communist and started distributing the party paper in the village when he went back there on weekends.

My father believed in Trotsky, in Lenin, in the Russians, in Yuri Gagarin, and in Valentina. He still remembers whole speeches by Nasser and can recite them by heart, even though there was only one radio in the village back then and everyone had to crowd around it to listen. To this day, the phrases *In the name of the nation* and *in the name of the people* are my father's favorites. My mother loved Nasser too. She was in high school when he died, and she always tells us how they carried a mock coffin through the village and held a mock funeral. My grandmother says the Jews put poison in his cigarettes. That he didn't just die, the way they say, it had all been planned.

My father says there's no comparing Nasser and Sadat. The day Sadat was killed, we were on our way home from Tulkarm. They announced it on the radio, and Father laughed. He said it was about time. He couldn't understand why Egypt had stopped fighting in '73. He even named my older brother Sam, after the Russian SAM missiles the Egyptians used in the October war. My father says Golda Meir had been on the verge of agreeing to surrender. It was all because of that sonofabitch King Hussein. Too bad Nasser didn't have him killed, my father says, and then he puts on an Egyptian accent and tells us how Nasser once said that Hussein was a dog: You step on his tail in London to make sure he'll bark in Amman.

My father doesn't understand how my brothers and I came out the way we did. We can't even draw a flag. He says kids much smaller than us walk through the streets singing "P-L-O—Israel, no!" and he shouts at us for not even knowing what PLO stands for.

Anemones

My parents got up early for work. My mother was first. Since I was always up before my brothers, I was in charge of getting the morning groceries: a loaf of bread and 100 grams of hard cheese. The grocery store was just across the way, but I preferred to run the errand as early as possible, because I didn't want to be stuck with the Gazazweh, the workers from Gaza, who showed up there every morning. I almost always did get stuck with them, though, and even the few times when I arrived early enough, I'd see them getting off their buses just as I was leaving. Their buses stopped right near the store, engines still running, and the workers would swoop down by the dozen. The store would fill up completely, with a long line outside too. I hated the Gazazweh because everyone hated them; I was afraid they'd kidnap me. They looked to me like ordinary people, and they never bothered anyone, but my grandma's stories about all the children who misbehaved, and whose parents sold them to the Gazazweh, had me really scared. I always saw myself getting on one of their red buses and standing in line with them outside the grocery store. You'd only see them early in the morning when it was still dark outside, be-

cause they weren't supposed to be moving about in the daytime. They came to buy food, and then they'd vanish as if they'd
never been there, as if there were no Gazazweh in the world.

When I returned with the groceries, Father was always in
the bathroom. That's where he'd smoke his morning cigarette,
which he'd put out in the cup of coffee he had in there. I always
went in after him and removed the cup with the cigarette butt.
A bathroom, after someone has had coffee and a cigarette in it,
has a special smell. My father had a special smell. I know that
smell of morning in the bathroom, know it very well. It wasn't
unpleasant. I liked it. I hardly saw Father in the morning because, right after his cigarette and coffee, he'd take his plastic
lunch box with the sandwiches Mother had made for him and
leave for work.

My father worked in a place he used to refer to as the
packinghouse or *Kalmaniyya.* I didn't know what it meant, but
I assumed my father picked fruit.

Jamal, our Hebrew teacher in grade school, never tired of
telling us about the fruit pickers. We spent more time hearing
him talk about fruit picking than about Hebrew. He kept yelling that we'd wind up as fruit pickers. "Like donkeys," he'd
say. "You'll leave home at six in the morning and get back late
at night."

He happened to like me, the teacher Jamal. I was the best
student in the class, and I did what I could to keep from becoming a fruit picker. But I was convinced nothing would help.
My grandma had worked as a fruit picker, my father was a fruit
picker, and I figured I'd become one too. I felt sorry for Father

and hoped that the teacher Jamal didn't know he worked at fruit picking too, leaving the house at 6 A.M. and returning late at night. Father had been the best student in his class too, and he had the nicest handwriting.

Unlike Father, Grandma talked a lot about her work as a fruit picker. She told us about Abu Ziad, our neighbor, who used to take the neighborhood widows in his pickup and let them off at the Mehadrin groves, where they'd alternate between picking oranges and picking pistachio nuts. She worked barefoot and liked to show us the cracked and hardened soles of her feet as proof. "Morning to night," she always told us. "Rain or shine, day in and day out, for one shilling a day." Grandma did all this for her children, but especially for Father, her only son, so he could study. But he destroyed it all and broke her heart. "It wasn't the fruit picking that finished off my legs and my back, but the grief your father gave me. God bless him, I have no one in the world besides him."

My grandmother started picking fruit after her husband was killed in the war. She was left on her own with four daughters and one son, who was two months old when he lost his father. Grandma always tells people how eagerly her husband had waited for a son, and when she tells this story she always takes the edge of her head scarf and dabs at a tear in her left eye. She was a hero in those days. When the Jews bombed Tira, she put her baby on a stack of wheat and bent over him. "I told myself it would be better if the shell hit me and not my son. As if it would have made any difference. It would probably have killed both of us anyway."

I tried to picture my grandma younger, but I couldn't. I always saw her as an old woman, just the way I knew her, with her faltering legs and her white dress, lying on top of that crying baby who didn't know he had no father, and I could picture the shells falling beside her in the wheat fields of Tira, and how only by some miracle she wasn't hurt. She gets up, grabs the baby, runs a little farther (until the plane comes back to drop some more bombs), and falls to the ground again. My grandma always says that if war breaks out we mustn't stay inside the house because it'll collapse on top of us. And we mustn't turn on the light. We'd better hide among the trees.

I loved picturing the wheat fields that my grandma used to talk about. I loved picturing the *baidar* too, the silo, and the people gathered there like it was an important holiday, tossing the wheat in the air with their pitchforks, so the grain would fall in one heap and the chaff would fly in the wind and form a separate one.

They used to be rich once. Three camels, carrying all sorts of valuable goods, would take the wheat and the vegetables from their fields in el-Bassah back to the house. They'd paid a shilling for each camel. Grandpa and Grandma had cows and horses too, and a trained dog that always sat on the balcony, to protect the poultry from the cats, and never tried to go indoors.

My grandpa was very smart. He could read and write, and he had a nice handwriting. But the schools back then weren't like the ones we have today. Otherwise, he would have studied medicine and become a doctor. Grandma says she could have become an engineer if they'd sent her off to study, but girls didn't go to school in her day. We always believed her when she said this. We thought she'd have made a good engineer. And the truth is, even though she never studied anything, she was a skillful card player, could do math—addition and subtraction—and knew where each plot of land ended and the next one began.

My grandpa, who had a little mustache, like he has in the only picture of him in Grandma's room, was a hero, a strong man who had fought against the Jews, but he died at the entrance to his own home just as he was picking some grapes. All he said was "Allah" and fell over. He'd taken a bullet. Grandma didn't understand why he'd fallen.

"I told him, Get up, *ya zalameh*, come on, get up. What's the matter with you?" She thought he was just pretending.

Grandma says Grandpa is a *shahid*, and there are anemones growing in the spot where he bled. She says Abu Ziad was eaten by worms when he died, but they didn't go near my grandfather. That's how it is: A *shahid*'s body doesn't rot. It stays just the way it was.

The Aden Hafla

My father was the first person in our neighborhood to buy a VCR. It was big and heavy, made of metal. The cassettes were different back then, short and thick. When we first got it, all our relatives dropped by. They came to congratulate us and brought bags of rice and big packets of coffee, and Father would put on *The Black Samurai* and *Amar Akbar Anthony*, an Indian film starring Amitabh Bachchan, about three brothers who are separated at birth after a bad guy kills their father. They're united in the end, and they get even with all the bad guys.

My father once brought home a movie called *The Aden Hafla*. We watched it over and over and over. The whole family would sit in front of the TV, watching it together. Grandma would sit closest, because her eyesight wasn't what it used to be. There were children with kaffiyehs and pistols, and musicians, and singers and poets. We knew the songs by heart. There was a little girl who sang her father a song before he went off to war, and Grandma would always wipe away a tear. Everyone would make the V-sign with their fingers before they got up to perform.

Father's friends came specially to watch the film. They cracked sunflower seeds and peered at the screen. Father always laughed at them when they didn't recognize someone. "What's with you? That's Abu-Jihad," or "You don't know who Mahmoud Darwish is?!" Once this friend of his thought that Al-Fakahani was the name of a grocer in Beirut, and Father made him leave.

At night he'd give the cassette to Grandma, and she'd hide it in her chicken coop. My mother couldn't stand Grandma's chickens, with the dirt they made, and the noise. There was a major battle between them because of those chickens, and they stopped talking to each other for a pretty long time. Me, I was all for Grandma's chickens. One day my mother burned down the small coop with the *Aden Hafla* tape inside. Father got mad and stormed off to play cards.

The next day, Father didn't come home from work. There were no phones back then, and Mother and Uncle Bashir took the Agrexco jeep and went looking for him. All my aunts arrived and started crying. I could hear them talking about fliers, about Land Day, and about detention.

Grandma spent the whole night on a straw mat under the eucalyptus trees in front of the house, crying and waiting. Mother didn't come home either; Grandma said she was with Father but didn't say where that was. The next day, my brothers and I stayed home from school. I sat on the mat under the tree with Grandma. She kept swaying. Her eyes were red and swollen, and she fixed them on the farthest point down the road. Whenever a car would drive up, she'd stop swaying and stiffen.

She followed each car with her eyes until it had gone by, and then she'd go back to swaying and staring.

Mother wanted to cut down the eucalyptus trees outside our house. She said they made a lot of dirt, and the entrance to the house looked ugly because of them. Grandma said that cutting them down would be a disaster, because eucalyptus trees contain a *wali*, a holy spirit who guards the home and the village. She told us how Grandpa's father, Sheikh Ahmad, used to stand beside the eucalyptus trees and talk with the rebels in Jaffa and in the mountains. He would warn them against the Jews, telling them where they were hiding and which route was safest.

Two days later, my father was released from detention. They'd picked him up at a roadblock on his way to a demonstration in Taiyiba. They'd searched the car and found the fliers. With the stubble on his cheeks, he looked very different. Grandma hugged him and kept on crying. "When will you learn, *yamma, ya habibi?*"

Cap Guns

I'd always known there would be a war. When I was little, my brothers and I dug trenches in the grove of fruit trees behind our house. We dug with our hands, which were small. We couldn't dig very deep, because pretty soon we hit ground that was too hard, and our attempts to soften it with water didn't help. We wanted to dig large trenches around the entire house, so we could hide there when the shooting started. Trenches that we could stand up straight in, and only Grandma and Father and Mother would have to bend over. We filled plastic bags with sand and stacked them to form a wall, just the way Grandma said they did in the war, but the bags didn't last. They fell apart within days.

Once Father took us up to another village, Ya'bad, to meet some people who worked with him in the packinghouse. They had a car with a green license plate, and Father said that was how the Jews marked them. The war in Ya'bad was very real, not like the one in Grandma's stories. There were bullet holes in the walls of Father's friends' homes. It really scared me, because it had never occurred to me that a bullet could actually make a hole through the wall and get inside the house. They had green iron doors with holes you could look through and see the living room.

Father said it wouldn't happen to us, because we were different. We believed him, because the people in Ya'bad talked differently, and also because our doors were made of wood.

Sometimes Father and Mother would load the four of us in the backseat, and we'd make the trip almost as far as Ya'bad, and then we'd go back home without seeing our friends. Half-way there, Father would turn around, swear, and say that we couldn't get through to Ya'bad that day because of a roadblock. He'd say that the people in Ya'bad and their children were heroes. They weren't spineless nothings like us.

My brothers and I were constantly playing war games. We'd be at it every day. At first, we used swords—I mean sticks—like in the movies about the wars of the Prophet Mohammed. I was Hamzah, the Prophet's uncle. He was very strong in the movies, and he had a sword with two blades. He would fight against ten infidels at once and kill them all. My older brother was Ali, the Prophet's cousin, and my two younger brothers were the khalifs Omar and Utman, the Prophet's deputies. Nobody could be the Prophet Mohammed. Grandma said if we did that we would go right to hell. They never showed the Prophet Mohammed in the movies either, only his camel and a halo of light above.

Later we started using pistols, like in the film by Omar el-Mukhtar in Libya and the one about Jamila Bukhird in Algiers. On 'id el-fitr and 'id el-adha, my father always took us to Tulkarm to buy us pistols. No child in our village had pistols as beautiful as ours: made of iron, almost real. Before the holiday, when our grocery store still sold cap guns, we'd play the real thing. When we ran out of ammunition, we'd shout "Bang, bang!" but whoever did the shooting had to pull the trigger too. Otherwise it didn't count and you weren't dead.

When we were growing up, Father would bring us *Rambo* and commando movies, and that's when we moved to heavy artillery. Our war games went out of the house and into the grove, spreading over the whole neighborhood. My older brother was the commander of one group, and I took the other. He never won, unless he cheated or unless one of the soldiers in my group abandoned his post and went off to pee.

When we were older we shifted to automatic weapons, big guns made of wood with a magazine and a trigger and a piece of string for slinging the weapon across your shoulder. We made everything ourselves. First we called all the guns Bren, a word we'd taken from Grandma's stories. But after watching *Azit the Paratrooper Dog* we started calling them Uzi. There was one that could shoot down seven Arabs at once, and my father got all worked up and told us it was an M-16 and could shoot sixty bullets a second. After that, no matter what weapon we had, we'd call it an M-16, even though none of us could shout *bang* sixty times in a second. So we switched from *bang* to *brrrrr.* I called my group Fedayeen and my older brother called his group Fedayeen too, because Father had always told us the Fedayeen were the best.

One day Father shouted to us to come home. We were in the middle of a game, and I was just about to kill my older brother, but Father shouted so loud we had no choice. We got the two younger ones from their positions and scurried home, because if Father lost it he was capable of hitting us. When we got home, he turned the volume up on the TV till it couldn't go any higher. Mother was crying, and my grandmother, who never cried, sounded like she was about to cry too.

"Look," my father ordered us, and kept saying, "*Yal'an Allah, yal'an Rabhoom, yal'an rab Allah* who made them." Grandma tore at her clothing and keened. My older brother and I were relieved nobody had hit us; we thought Father must have brought home a new film he wanted us to see. The next day we went back to our war games. My brother called his group Sabra and I called mine Chatilla.

Scouts

Once, I got up on a stage in a *kaffiyeh*. I must have been in the third grade at the time. A man with an accent showed up at school with my father. Father left, and the man with the accent took me in his car to a house I'd never seen before. A pretty house, big, with enormous sofas and lots of potted plants and plastic flowers. He took out a piece of paper with sentences in Arabic that I didn't understand and said I'd be opening the Jafra Festival that evening. He asked me to memorize the sentences and taught me how to make the V-sign with my fingers.

That night they put the *kaffiyeh* on me and placed me up on a stage with some musicians. I recited my lines, which had lots of references to *wattan* (homeland) in them. My voice was shaking, and I was very stiff. I'd never seen so many people, all looking at me and listening to me. When I finished, I walked off the stage with my fingers in a V, and everyone applauded. My father was waiting for me backstage, and he smiled as I ran toward him to hide. The man with the accent smiled too and told me something I couldn't make out. Father said I was good.

Father sent me to the Scouts and said when I grew up I'd be a pilot, that by the time I finished high school we'd have our own state, and I could study to become a pilot then. Grandma said I'd be a minister or a judge. In the Scouts, we spent all our time playing soccer, and when one of the teachers at our school died, they would take us to stand beside his grave. Only those who had a uniform could stand by the grave, so my father took me to Tulkarm to buy me khaki pants, a green shirt, and fabric for making ties.

While we were inside the clothing store, we heard shouting outside. The owner asked us to leave and pulled down the iron bars at the front of the store. In the street across the way, older children with flags were blocking the road with tires. My father left me near the car and ran toward them with a lighter. I started crying. I was sure it was the end of the world, like they taught us in Koran lessons. My father said he couldn't believe I was such a coward. And if I was, what was the point of all my I-want-a-gun?

My grandfather had a gun. Grandma says he was a brave fighter who had tried to defend Tira. She says the Jews couldn't get inside the village, and it wasn't until the Arabs handed us over that they came in. But Father says it was lucky for us King Abdullah handed the village over to the Jews in time, because otherwise they would have slaughtered us one by one.

When Grandpa's son from his first wife was killed, Grandpa wanted to take revenge. Akab had been a real hero, one of the Rebels. He'd had a horse, a gun, and a belt full of grenades. One Friday, he took a bullet. The bullet hit the belt, and all

31

the grenades went off at once. His body scattered in every direction. Grandma says the whole family worked till nightfall to gather up his head and his shoulders, so they would have something to bury. He had a face as round as the full moon.

Grandma says that at night, after the burial, my grandfather went up on the roof of the school building. There was an Iraqi outpost there and they'd take turns behind the Bren hidden in the bags of sand. Grandpa heard the Jews coming closer. He heard the commander say "Forward, forward"— Grandma whispered the word in Hebrew. The first bullet hit the commander, the one who'd said "Forward," and Grandpa saw the Jews in a state of panic, trying to get away. Grandpa put the Bren to good use and sewed them together "like a Singer." "They're cowards, the Jews, but the British, those Ingliz dogs, preferred them," my grandmother says.

The Ingliz got into Grandpa and Grandma's house once. That was before my father was born. They turned everything upside down: spilled salt on the sugar, smashed bowls, and peed right in front of her. Grandma says one of them sat on the big container of olives and took a shit right into it. They poured everything out afterward, and saw the Englishman's shit, big chunks.

The People in Tira
Used to Be Braver

T he people in Tira used to be braver and kept all the Jews out. Once, some Jews tried to get into the village by pretending to be Arabs. They came with *kaffiyehs.* But Abu el-Abed knew they were Jews. He'd been working in the wheat fields with his family, and he'd seen them. When he told the people around him that they were Jews, they thought he'd gone crazy. "What's got into you. They're the Iraqi soldiers," they told him.

But Abu el-Abed was certain he was right. He could tell Jews by the way they walked. He told his friends, "One shot in the air, and we'll know. If they're Arabs, they'll shout to us; if they're Jews, they'll lie down flat on the ground." As soon as he fired, they all went down in the dust. It was obvious that they were Jews. Abu el-Abed and the other men stayed there, shooting and scaring them, and the women and children hurried home, shouting in the streets, *"Ya ahl al-balad, al-Yahud akhduna!"* ("People of the village, the Jews have come to occupy us!")

All the men went out. Handsome, brave, unwavering, as if they were going to a wedding. The women accompanied them with *za'aruta,* the traditional cries of happiness. They hardly had any guns. They held sticks and knives, stones and spades, and wouldn't let any Jew come near. That day, they managed to seize three bodies of Israeli soldiers.

Abu el-Abed and some of the fighters in Tira tied them to horses and dragged them to the Iraqi army headquarters in Tulkarm. They wanted to prove it was possible to kill Jews. Their aim was to encourage the Arab soldiers and persuade them to fight. But the Iraqis said, "*Maku awamer, maku slakh*" ("We have no orders, we have no ammunition").

One time they were even braver than that and wouldn't let Kahana in. We heard on the news that he was planning to come to Tira. They announced on the mosque loudspeakers: "*Ya ahl al-balad,* Kahane is arriving tomorrow to take back the released prisoners. If he gets in, it will be our disgrace."

By five the following morning, I was already out with my father at the entrance to the village from the direction of Kfar Sava and Ramat Ha Kovesh. There were some people there blocking the roads with tires. Father said the workers shouldn't be allowed out. He said everyone had to defend the village, and that when the Jews lose out on a day of work, they get furious. "Do you know how much we're making them lose by not going to work?"

Police vans drew up, and my father and a few other people sat down in the middle of the road. I wasn't scared. I sat down with them. The mayor spoke with the policemen, and they moved back. Soon the entire village had rallied. Thousands blocked the entrance. An airplane circled overhead, and Father said they were taking pictures of us from the air. He pulled his shirt up over his face and taught me how to do it too, just like the kids you see on TV.

That day Father and I were late coming home. Mother and Grandma were very worried. They waited under the eucalyptus trees at the front of the house. I felt like a man. I wasn't afraid. But all they wanted was to make sure my father was all right. They didn't even ask me what had happened.

Nothing *had* happened actually. Kahane didn't come. At school the next day the kids said they'd broken the windows of the police vans with bricks, and they said Kahane had come into the village that night through the orange groves of Tel Mond, dressed as a woman.

A Third-Year Student

My father wrote that the holiday meant nothing to him. That it didn't evoke the least emotion. That his real holiday hadn't come yet, and that when it did he wouldn't be the only one to rejoice; everyone would rejoice. He also wrote that there was a special Visitors' Day for the holiday and that, as a one-time exception, visitors might bring in a kilo of holiday sweets.

The postcards were sent from Damon prison, P.O. Haifa, March 1970. He had been in jail for a year by then. I know because there's also a copy of *Ha'aretz* from March 1969 in the suitcase, with an item about my father's being arrested. It links him to the explosion in the Hebrew University cafeteria.

According to the letters and the papers, my father was in jail for more than two years. There's a thick layer of dust over the papers. Inside Father's matriculation certificate, I found a dried spider. His grades weren't that good, but he always says that the grades in his day didn't come close to the ones we get nowadays, and that someone who got a 70 back then was smarter than someone who gets 100 today. Grandma kept all his report cards. She can't read, but she knows what's important. Up to ninth grade he had only hundreds. The comments at the bottom said he should try to settle down, to be good, to be less noisy. The report card at the end of eleventh grade says: *Promoted to twelfth grade on condition that he obeys the rules.*

Sometimes I think nobody except Grandma and me knows about the letters, the newspaper clippings, and those report cards. Judging by the dust, I must be the only other person to look at them. I rummage through the papers, sorting them by date, by place, by institution, and put them down next to my grandmother.

She doesn't even notice me. I have to position myself directly in front of her and shout my name in her ear before she realizes that I should get a hug and a kiss. She sits there, rocking, in front of the heater, fingering her prayer beads, listening to Voice of Amman, and waiting for the next call of the muezzin.

In all his letters from prison, Father wrote to Grandma too. "Tell my dear mother" or "This is for my beloved mother" or "Tell the dearest person of all." He usually sent the letters to his brothers-in-law, my aunts' husbands. In all of them, he sounded all right—or at least as if he was trying to sound all right. In October 1969, in the oldest postcard I found, he said that the problems of adjusting to life in jail were behind him. There were people you wouldn't usually have a chance to meet, and he got along well with them. In one of the letters, he told Uncle Bashir he was slowly turning into an *abu-ali*, a big shot.

In a later letter, after a sixth-month remand, he wrote about the wonderful library and said he spent all his time there, studying.

> Tell my dear mother I'm very glad they gave me another six months. Tell her I asked them to, because there are books here that I haven't had a chance to read yet. There are so many books, and I spend every minute in the library, except if someone asks me to play some chess. Please ask Mother to bring me an English-Hebrew dictionary from home.

When they prolonged his detention again, he wrote that five years wouldn't be enough for him to finish all the books he'd listed for himself. He talked about the unusual opportunity he'd been given to purify his body and soul and to test his endurance and resolve. He knew now that he'd been born to be a prisoner. He could not imagine himself without the bars and the barbed wire.

> Were it not for the fact that you and my sisters miss me, I would stay here forever. I like it here. The only thing that disturbs me is that you did everything you could in order for me to reach the top. I feel sad for every drop of perspiration you shed on my behalf. I know I've let you down. The only thing missing in my life now is the opportunity to make it up to you. I don't know how.

In one of the papers that has turned completely yellow, the picture of my father is no more than a blur and I can hardly make it out. They don't write anything interesting. Just his picture and his name with the caption: *A third-year student.* Judging by his grades in the first two years, it looks like he wasn't particularly brilliant or diligent. He didn't take too many courses. One of them was Nationalist Movements in Modern Times, with Professor Y. Talmon. It seems he didn't put too much of an effort into his university career, just like me. When I dropped out, I was so ashamed of myself that I didn't dare go home. But it didn't occur to me to blow up the cafeteria.

My father was twenty-two when he was arrested. He thought at the time that he was twenty-three. Grandma kept a letter she had sent to the editor of *Al-Quds.* They published it under the heading RELEASE MY SON. She wrote that she was a widow whose husband had died twenty-three years earlier, leaving her with four daughters and a son. She'd done everything she could for them, her son was the very essence of her life, and she was asking the Minister of Police, the Minister of Defense, and the Prime Minister to release him. The headline of the story above the letter announced that the village of Arabeh would be hooked up to electricity in the course of 1970.

After that, Grandma went on a hunger strike, and father wrote another postcard to Uncle Bashir, urging him to make her stop. If he'd been suffering, that's one thing, but he was really doing fine in jail. Genuinely fine. He was chess champion of his whole wing.

My father doesn't talk about those days. All I know is what the papers reported or the things he himself wrote in his letters, which don't explain much either. In 1971, the Council of Arab Students circulated a handbill denouncing the policy of administrative detentions and demanding that Father be put on trial or released immediately. It said the police had closed the cafeteria bombing case and all those involved had been tried.

The Dead Sea

I went to the Dead Sea once, with my grandmother. It's good for you if you have aches in your legs. She asked her friend Amneh to sign me up for the trip too. Amneh was a tour organizer who specialized in trips for women, mainly older women her own age. Sometimes they'd go to the Hamat-Gader spa, sometimes to Jerusalem for Friday prayers. She organized trips to any place that could help people's bones.

Grandma and Amneh had been friends all the way back, since the time of the Ingliz. Amneh's husband had a gun that the English had given him to defend the village. One day when Amneh's husband went indoors to sleep and left his gun beside him, Abu Ziad, that scoundrel, came inside and stole it. The English thought Amneh's husband had sold the gun. Two soldiers held his legs up with a stick, and the officer struck the soles of his feet with a whip. They didn't believe the gun had been stolen. They stripped him and whipped him across the back. His cries could be heard as far as the fields, and the whole village came running to see what had happened. Only when the English were about to shoot Amneh's husband did Abu Ziad intervene and tell them he'd found the gun in the field. Liar.

Amneh looked like my grandmother: the same white dresses meant for outings, the same white scarf covering her head. They were the oldest women on that trip to the Dead Sea. The others were all younger. Every once in a while, my grandma pointed gently at one of them and asked Amneh, "Whose daughter is she? She's sweet. Why isn't she married?" The whole way there on the bus, the women kept playing the *darabukka,* singing, and dancing. One of them held the microphone and sang an Indian song from the movie *Kurbani,* which was a hit at the time. Everyone knew the words and sang along with her.

I walk in the middle, with Grandma holding my right hand and Amneh holding my left. They're sorry they haven't taken their walking sticks. The bus trip has tired them out, and it's very hot. All the women have gone into the sea already, and we're the last ones to reach the shore. A few of the girls are laughing at us, but Grandma and Amneh can't see or hear from such a distance.

I don't mind their laughing at us. I stick with the two of them. I love listening to their stories, things nobody else knows. They keep repeating the same ones. About how people shot themselves in the arm to avoid being drafted into the Turkish army to fight in their war. The Turks would take them far into the mountains, where there was snow, and they would die of the cold. Nobody made it back alive.

Grandma and Amneh remove their white dresses. They're wearing less fancy white dresses underneath, the kind that can be worn in the water. And under those they have their *sharwals.*

They walk haltingly toward the water, afraid of slipping. They decide to sit down on the stones and inch their way in. I sit in the middle, holding their hands and inching my way in too.

Once we reach the water, Grandma wants me to come in, but I stay where I am so I can see her and make sure she doesn't get lost. I watch over her from a distance. I'll go in afterward, when she's out. Their white dresses float on the water and look like two parachutes. Everyone laughs. Me too. It's the first time I see my grandmother in the water. I can picture her now, young and strong. I can picture her working in the fields.

Once people in the village would fall in love in the fields. Sometimes Grandma would tell me about how a man and a woman we knew had met in the wheat field, and how another couple would exchange glances by the well at the edge of the village. She herself never did things like that. When she was young, she rode a horse from Qalqiliya to Tira. She loved riding horses, and she dressed as a man, covering her head with a *kaffiyyeh* and galloping off. Two riders followed her for quite a distance, but they couldn't catch up with her. They couldn't believe it when they discovered the rider was a woman, but she brushed them off, yelled it was none of their business, and rode back home.

Grandma was an orphan. Her mother died giving birth to her, and her father died shortly after that. She and her two brothers grew up with their uncle, her father's older brother. Her aunt and uncle were good people. First they fed the orphans and only then did they feed themselves. They kept the orphans' land safe and gave them what they had coming. They had a good life, better than the lives of children in the village who hadn't lost their father.

My grandma didn't know my grandpa, her husband, at all. She hadn't met him in the fields or "any of that nonsense." She curses him sometimes when she recalls how he took her. *Al-shahib* (the white-haired one) she'd call him. He was married then, and he had grown children. His two older daughters were married already. Grandma's brother wanted to marry Grandpa's third daughter, so Grandpa asked for Grandma in return. It's known as *badal* (exchange marriage). You give me yours, I'll give you mine. You protect my honor, I'll protect yours. And she was a mean woman, Grandpa's third daughter. She had her mind set on making my grandmother's life miserable for marrying her father, as if she wanted to keep him to herself.

Once Grandpa hit Grandma because of her. The third daughter had come to his house and cried, "Father, Father, my husband hit me; he threw me out of the house." It was all a lie, as it turned out afterward, but after what? After Grandpa gave Grandma a beating. Because that's how it is with the *badal*. You hit that one, I'll hit this one. You throw yours out of the house, I'll throw mine out of the house. That's how you keep your wives in check. It's a kind of guarantee.

"But he was good to you," Amneh tells her, and jabs her with her knee. "Why don't you mention how he used to take you on his shoulders, like my husband did, *Allah yerakhamu*? Why don't you mention how he took you to Jaffa once, to the theater, to see singers perform?" Amneh turns to me and says, "Your grandfather put a tarbush on her head, gave her some men's clothing, and took her to see singers. What woman in the village got to see singers perform back then? Forgot about that, didn't you, you dried-out old woman? He used to take you everywhere on his horse." And she gives Grandma another jab. Grandma smiles and mumbles something, and Amneh continues, "Without him, we wouldn't even have known there was such a thing as the Dead Sea."

Five Little Blocks

If not for that picture of a face and shoulders, a man of about forty, with a little mustache and a blue jacket over a white shirt, there would be nothing left to remember my grandfather by. Sometimes my grandmother would tell me he was a hero, and sometimes she'd say he was just an old rake who'd abducted her from her aunt and uncle's home when she was young.

On holidays, when we were very little, Grandma used to take us to the cemetery near the house. Almost everyone in the village would go, because that's how it is: On the mornings of holidays you go to the cemetery. My father never came with us to visit his father. Grandfather's grave was small and plain, less ornate than the others. The cemetery was full of people, and all of them were sitting around crying, alongside big white beautiful tombs. There were flowers on all of them. Some had little turrets, like the ones you find in a mosque. There were gravestones with three or four tiers. My older brother said that four tiers meant sheikhs or people who would definitely get into heaven directly, no questions asked, the way we'd been taught in religion classes. Each holiday the graves grew bigger. They started building them out of marble and ceramic. My older brother would roam about, looking for new ones, and he'd check to see if the dead really did come back. I was afraid to move too far away from Grandma. She said you must never step on the stones, because all of them had been graves once. I was careful and looked a million times before taking a step. I clenched Grandma's flowing white dress, to make sure I didn't get lost among all those people. I didn't step on the smallest stones either, because I thought those might be the graves of children. My grandmother said little children don't die. God simply picks them out and gathers them to him, because he wants to turn them into angels.

Five little blocks are covered in weeds. In winter the weeds grow high and green, and in summer they are yellow and dry. My grandmother bends the branches, exposing the blocks (which are covered in a thick layer of sand), sits down beside the grave, and starts reciting verses from the Koran. She says she knows plenty of verses, even though she's never studied. Later, when the old men in the mosque start reading the holiday verses over the loudspeakers, everyone starts shaking hands and handing out money and candy to the children. Some kids in my class managed to collect enough money to buy ten pistols. All they had to do was to say *Allah yerakhamu*. Only boys would come to the cemetery to collect holiday money. Girls never did.

Grandma would change some bills in the grocery store and bring a bagful of coins with her to hand out to the kids. She gave out a lot of money, and I would get upset with her for not giving it all to me. I know those kids, I'd tell her. They don't deserve any of it.

Grandma never allowed us to take money from people, though some of them would hand us coins even without our saying *Allah yerakhamu.* Grandma wouldn't let us take cakes either, although the older women who looked just like her used to beg her to take a small slice in honor of the Prophet Mohammed. Grandma always responded politely and warmly. She kissed their hands, wished peace on the soul of their loved one in heaven, and didn't take a thing.

I wouldn't take anything either. I believed my grandmother when she said you shouldn't take anything in a graveyard. She said we didn't need anything, and that only the children who'd been bad would do it. She loved to take us along and kept saying that this way at least we would know where Grandpa was buried. Not like my father, who behaved as if it weren't his father.

On Our Way
to the Sea

My father used to tell us about Grandpa too some times, especially on our way to the sea. Father had some set stories for car trips. Near Ramat Ha Kovesh he would always laugh and tell us again about Uncle Mahmoud's accident and about how his new Dodge had been totaled. In Kfar Sava he would point to a small building and tell us that the Shabak was under there, and he had been there several times for interrogations. The interrogators had begged him to tell them what people were saying in the cafés, that's all—but he wouldn't. And when we'd go to the sea and pass by the cemetery of Tel Mond, he'd always remind us that all the tombstones bore the inscription 1948, THE BATTLE FOR TIRA. He said we had to believe him because he'd actually been there and had seen for himself what they said.

Without fail, Father always repeated those same stories whenever we drove by. He'd remind us that, to this very day, Tel Mond and Ramat Ha Kovesh won't have anything to do with us, because we killed so many of their people. That he didn't know how many Grandpa had killed, but he figured it had to be quite a few, because Grandpa was a fighter, even though he didn't die in battle. He would always end the story with the promise that someday he'd stop and show us around the Tel Mond cemetery. We went to the beach almost every week. We never stopped there.

Grandma didn't want us to go to the sea. She kept warning Father, suggesting that we go to the mountains instead; she said that for the same price he could light a fire and barbecue a few chickens for the children. She was always on edge as she waited for us to come back, and she didn't stop worrying until she saw us herself. When we drove up the street, she would stiffen and try to count the passengers even before we'd parked. Grandma always said the sea was dangerous; even if we stayed close to the beach there was a chance that a deep well would form suddenly and suck us in. Her second stepson had drowned in the sea.

But she also told us that as a little girl she would go to the beach all the time. She said all of Tira went; the lands of the village stretched as far as the sea. She didn't go in deep, just enough to wet her feet. People used to come to the beach with camels loaded down with watermelons. Delicious big watermelons, better than anything you can get nowadays. Every few meters there was someone with a stack of watermelons. Strangers who spoke a language that only the big men could understand would arrive to buy the watermelons. They had lots of workers, who carried the melons for them and loaded them onto their ships.

Grandma used to ride there on the back of a donkey, with her uncles and their children. They'd use the money from the watermelons to buy clothes in Qalqiliya. Everyone got the same thing—same quantity, same colors—to make sure nobody could say, "You got more." Everything was different back then. Nobody tried to cheat you, and people weren't scary. The only scary things were the jackals and the wolves.

On holidays, they'd go to the Sidna-Ali Mosque. The men would slaughter sheep for an offering, and the women would light a fire and roast them. Grandma says that only the city women, who spoke differently and dressed like sluts, would go into the sea. They weren't embarrassed, they were like my mother, who thinks she's young and walks around with her hair uncovered. The city women didn't cook, and the farm women would feed them and enjoy poking fun at them. Crazy ladies.

Land

When my grandfather was killed, Grandma left home. Her stepchildren, who were older than she was, wanted the house, and she gave it up in return for some land. There was plenty of land back then, and they had no problem giving her two dunams of wheat fields in exchange. My grandmother says, "They threw me out, with my small children. Four girls and a baby boy still in swaddling cloth. Now they want the land. Let them go on dreaming."

Nowadays everyone fights over an extra ten centimeters of land. Grandma's stepchildren's children claim that the distribution wasn't fair, and they want her to give them half a dunam. But Grandma won't budge. She gets up, bares her fingernails, and fights for her land. What the Jews took from her was bad enough. She takes the papers in their plastic wrapping out of the blue suitcase and mutters, "This is my deed for the land, and this is the one for the lands in the field. It's all written here, with maps and lawyers' signatures and everything. They thought I was stupid, that I'd simply take them at their word. But I got everyone to sign back then."

Grandma goes to city hall and asks them to make ten photocopies of her documents. She collects all the arguments that prove her right to the land and lashes out at her step-grandchildren, reminding them of everything she had to go through when she was made to live in a tent. She shouts at them that nobody gave her the land out of sheer kindness or love. She throws the papers at them, with all the maps and the signatures and the red ribbons of the Land Registry Bureau. "Get an engineer. We'll split the costs, and if I owe you anything, then *tfadallu*, be my guests."

They always back off in the end, with Grandma emerging the victor, but bleeding. They've insulted her; they've brought up things she's been trying to forget. The stepdaughter of the *badal* has left a scratch on her heart. My grandmother never cries, but her voice sometimes becomes choked with sorrow. "Did I let her brothers go hungry? May God never forgive her, in this world or the next."

Grandma yells at my father that he doesn't know how to stand up to those nothings. He's scared of a few self-important thugs. Can't protect his land, doesn't appreciate its value.

Sometimes my grandmother dreams about a place she calls el-Bassah, where her parents used to spend the sunny season. They didn't spray the watermelons there, just used fertilizer from the hens. She dreams of the camels they used to ride for three *grush* a person. After the war she went there once with a sack of straw on her head. The children were hungry, and she was going to see if there was anything left in the fields. They wouldn't let her go near. "*Rukh min hon,*" they told her. "*There's no land.* Go away." She tried to get past the soldier, but he pointed a gun at her chest.

When the Soviet Union was a superpower, my father used to say the lands would be returned someday. He taught us about Russian planes and tanks and antiaircraft missiles, Russian boats and submarines. "The Russians aren't like those spoiled Americans you see undressing in the movies. They're disciplined. The soldiers are well trained. They would never abandon their positions." He told us about one Russian who banged his shoe on the table at the United Nations and threatened the United States and Israel.

Father forced us to follow the Olympic Games and to root for the Russians. The Olympics are like a war, my father used to say. Anyone who wins in sports will win in airplanes too. The Russians always had the lead, and we had no doubt who would win. In those days, people had hope. In our village there were two girls called Valentina. In Kalansawa, someone named his oldest son Castro. To this day, they call him Abu-Castro.

Meanwhile, Father's dream had turned sour. He continued to root for the soccer teams in red but stopped following the Olympics. Hope gave way to despair, and the volumes of Marx and Lenin were relegated to the top shelf, to be replaced by the Yellow Pages in Hebrew and Arabic.

My father says, "*Al-ard zai al-ard*"—"The land is like honor." Anyone who sells his land sells his honor. But they pay $5,000 for every dunam of land that once belonged to the absentees. If Grandma has thirty dunams, that works out to

$150,000. It's a hefty sum, but land mustn't be sold. Especially considering that $5,000 for a dunam is actually nothing. There's a whole industry of attorneys handling the lands. Everyone in the village is selling. "I don't understand how they can sell. Not that it will ever revert to us. Or maybe it will, who knows. But it's a matter of principle."

My father understands about politics, watches the news, and reads the papers religiously. He leaves the radio on next to him even when he's asleep. He looks a wreck. He's come to realize it's never going to work out, and the way things are going, they're liable to take away even the land we still have left. He turns to us, his four sons, and says, "You're bound to leave. None of you is going to stay to defend the land. Refugees. Is that what you want to be? Look at what happened to the ones who ran away. It would be better to die than to run. But you, what do you know about the value of land?"

PART TWO

The Bump on My Head

The Craziest Kid
in the Village

My parents say that before I jumped off the roof and cracked my skull, I was the craziest kid in the village. They were worried about my future and did everything they could to set me straight, but nothing helped. My parents were shattered. I made their lives miserable. Not only theirs, the whole neighborhood's and all our relatives' lives too.

My father says everyone hated me; they couldn't stand the sight of me. Little kids didn't dare walk down the street in front of our house. He says neighbors filed complaints with the police on account of me. They thought of having me committed or putting me in reform school when I was not even in kindergarten yet.

My parents think back on it sometimes and laugh when they recall how I used to wake up before everyone else, jump out through the window, and head for the school near our house to look for bottles and bongs left behind by the *hashashin*, the hashish addicts. Then I'd run through the fields looking for cars that the car thieves had burned at night, and I'd come home with the charred license plates.

My father says by the time I was four everyone knew I'd grow up to be a car thief and a junkie. He says that on holidays, when the Tira delinquents stole the fanciest cars, I'd sneak out of the house and wait for them at the entrance to the village with all the *hashashin* and the worst kids, to cheer the drag racers. My father says the holidays became a nightmare because he spent the whole time chasing me up and down the streets.

My mother says that every Saturday, when she went to visit her parents, she'd tie my foot to something so I couldn't run away. She says that otherwise I'd have run off to chase cats, turn over garbage cans, knock on doors, and ring every doorbell along the way. She says I was the reason my father had to sell half a dunam of land and buy a car. Cars were expensive back then, but they had no choice; they had to find a reasonable way to take me to the pediatrician in Kfar Sava. Mother says the first bus ride was enough for her. When the driver stopped the bus and told us to get off because of something I'd done, she cried.

My older brother's body is full of scars. My parents point to a scar on his stomach and say, "That's from when you tried to operate on his stomach." They point to some large ones on his legs and tell me they're from when I decided to attach his left foot to his right leg and vice versa.

My parents say I broke three new television sets, and they had to buy new dishes almost every week. I broke the locks on the kitchen cabinets, I stopped up the toilet with sand, I slaughtered the neighbors' chickens, I put ants in my cousins' eyes, and I burned down half the mango grove. I had a complete stock of slingshots, but instead of stones I'd use nails, aiming at cars or at people who happened to be walking by.

My parents stopped going to relatives' weddings because of me. They hardly slept in those days, for fear of what I was liable to do at night. People felt sorry for them. Everyone figured there was something wrong with me.

Nothing frightened me. I wasn't afraid of kids or adults, belts or snakes. When they hit me I'd pretend to cry, and I'd apologize, promising it was the last time, and within two minutes something else would break, another calamity would happen. That was my biggest problem: I knew how to put on a good act. I'd writhe in pain and pretend I was dying, so they'd feel sorry for me and let me go.

My parents tried everything. They tried being nice, being tough, hitting me with a belt, with a stick, with their hands, spanking me, hitting me on the back, on the legs. They tried regular doctors and pills and sheikhs and medicine men, but when all is said and done, it was the bump on my head that did the trick.

It happened when our neighbor, Aisha, and her husband, Abu-Ibrahim, got divorced. That day she brought all her things from her house to our yard—a mattress and blankets, pillows and clothes—and waited for the truck. There was a whole pile of soft things there. When I saw the pile, I climbed up on building blocks I'd brought over from a construction site, grabbed hold of the water pipes, and used them to hoist myself up onto the roof. Then I tried to jump onto Aisha's pile of bedding and clothes. I missed and cracked my skull. They thought I was dead.

Father's shirt was soaked in blood, as he and Abu-Yakkan from the grocery store rushed me to the hospital. No one who saw me lying there on the stones, with the blood and everything, thought I'd make it. But me, I was like a monkey, back on my feet after a few days.

My parents say I didn't remember hitting my head or anything else that I had done before that. They say the bump on my head turned me into a human being. I'd broken my skull, but my brain was intact. Lucky for me I had a head as hard as stone. For two days, I lay there unconscious, but when I came to I was a different person—a wonderful child, polite and quiet and smart. On my very first evening home from the hospital I put on my pajamas and brushed my teeth, and at six o'clock I kissed my parents good night.

The Day I Saw Jews Up Close for the First Time

The day I saw Jews up close for the first time I wet my pants. Mother was furious, because she'd asked us to keep our clothes clean. She'd dressed us in our best outfits that morning, because she knew that when she got home from work in the evening she'd barely have enough time to cook before the guests arrived. So she'd dressed me up and sent me off to kindergarten.

The kindergarten teachers had decided to take us to the soccer field that day. They brought sunflower seeds for themselves, sat on the bleachers, and started chatting. The kids romped all over the field, fell down, and played ball. The girls played in the sand and threw bags of sand and little stones at one another. The teachers went on cracking sunflower seeds and relaxing, and from time to time they'd pounce on one of the kids and yell at him.

I knew I shouldn't join the games. I wasn't going to get my clothes dirty, not today. I was wearing blue overalls and a white shirt underneath. White gets dirty very quickly. I knew it was my best outfit, my new one. If I got it dirty, they wouldn't let me see the Jews who worked with my father.

I needed to pee, but I knew I could never pull down my overalls in front of the teachers and the rest of the kids. I saw other kids doing it, but I couldn't. I held back a little longer. It started hurting. I never cried so hard in my life. I had wet my pants. I couldn't hide it. Everyone saw.

One of the kids started laughing and ran off to tell the teacher. She didn't spank me, because she felt sorry for me. I cried hard, I screamed, and I rubbed my eyes with my fists. To this day I can feel the tears and the runny nose, the stinging in my eyes and the wet lower part of my overalls, rubbing against my feet and making it hard for me to walk.

One of the teachers, a teacher's aide in fact, dragged me by the hand back to school. She held her hand all the way out, to keep me as far from her as possible, and her expression was one of sheer disgust. "You should be ashamed of yourself," she told me. "You're a big boy already." My arm hurt. She took me to my older brother's class, the first grade, and pulled him out of class. All the kids heard her say he'd have to take me home because I'd wet my pants.

My screaming grew louder as my brother grabbed my hand and pulled me behind him. He was happy to get out of school early. He laughed at me, glad I'd gotten into trouble. "The Jews from Father's work will see you." He laughed. "Mother will kill you." As if I didn't know.

I don't remember whether I saw the Jews that day or not, but I don't think Mother spanked me. I think she restrained herself. All I remember is that after they left, she unwrapped the present they brought. It was chocolates. I remember her saying: "Is that all they brought? And we've been preparing for a solid week!"

Five years later, when I was in fourth grade, the Hebrew teacher came to class with an *ajnabi*, a Westerner, a stranger— blond, tall, good-looking, not like us. The teacher translated the stranger's Hebrew. He was from Seeds of Peace. We were in Seeds of Peace too from now on, and we'd be meeting with Jews. They'd come to us, and we'd go to them.

We liked the idea. Jews meant days off from school. And the teachers would behave better. They wouldn't hit us, and they'd smile all the time. The Jews had more women teachers. We only had one, and she was old. The Jews were coming from Kfar Sava.

The Hebrew teacher told each of us who our Jewish friend would be. Our class was bigger than the Jewish one, so sometimes two kids had to share. I got Nadav Epstein. We were supposed to take our friend home.

The whole village knew the Jews were coming. A week before the visit, each of us got a letter asking our parents to be prepared, not to do anything that would embarrass us, to make a good impression. My mother took the day off, so she'd have enough time to cook and straighten the house. She only had two classes that day anyway, and she made arrangements for a substitute. The women and the children who didn't go to school came outdoors early to wait for the Jews. My mother prepared a meat *seniyyeh* with *tehini, maklubah, melukhiyyeh* with chicken, and a salad. She set the table, bought a potted plant made of plastic, and dressed up.

Nadav was okay. I didn't know much Hebrew, but he was okay. Nice. What I didn't understand was why he called our loaves of bread *pitta*. In Tira, *pitta* is what you call a roll. The bread that the Jews call *pitta* we call bread.

Two weeks later we went to Kfar Sava to visit them, while a second group of Jews went to Tira. Their school looked completely different. They had loudspeakers in the yard, and they listened to music during recess. I saw a boy and girl walking arm in arm and waited for someone to hit them. I looked for Nadav and realized they'd made a mistake. The class they'd sent to Tira today was the same one that had visited already.

They paired us off, a Jew and an Arab. Some Jews got two Arabs. They matched me up with someone new. I didn't even ask his name. Pretty soon we figured out that the Jews weren't taking us to their homes. They'd prepared food for us at school; they'd set a table with loaves of Yahud bread, chocolate bars, and jam.

I didn't eat anything. I felt let down. How dare they give me a new friend? After my father had finally managed to teach me how to pronounce Epstein properly. The Arabs stood on one side, the Jews on the other. I was on the verge of tears, but I decided to hold back. I was upset with myself for caring which Jew they brought me. As if I'd even understood what Nadav had been talking about. Nobody really cared anyway. I bet Nadav didn't even notice they'd switched classes. Our teachers kept mumbling about the food. They'd been sure the Jews would take us home, and now they realized they'd dressed up for nothing.

Suddenly our principal came running over, all upset and perspiring, trying to fix his hair as he ran. He came directly to me. "Come on," he said. "They sent the wrong class. I'm taking you back to Tira with me." I never would have believed I'd actually get to ride in the principal's car. The principal told me that Nadav wouldn't stop crying because they'd switched classes. He refused to go with anyone but me. He screamed like a little child, the principal said. "He has a real problem, that kid. You've got to calm him down," he added. He'd wanted to take Nadav home, but the vice principal said it wouldn't be nice to take a Jewish boy home crying.

I was so happy. Nadav felt the same way I did. That Jew really did love me.

Taftish
(*Inspection*)

The geography teacher was the scariest teacher and the strongest. Once he grabbed Yakub by the ears and swung him in the air. Yakub was the biggest boy in the class. His legs hovered in midair and twisted around, and then the teacher hurled him against the blackboard. *Bang!*

We didn't say a word. We froze. Then a few kids laughed at Yakub.

The Arabic teacher would come in, make the rounds of our desks, and check to see who had done their homework. Invariably, half the class hadn't done it. They couldn't even read or write, so how could they do homework? She had a metal ruler, and anyone who hadn't done his homework would be tapped on the head and made to stand with his face up against the blackboard.

When she'd finished her inspection, they all lined up in front of her, well drilled, never complaining. They didn't try to get away or talk their way out of it, because they knew anyone who tried to pull anything would get a double dose. They would bow their heads, shut their eyes, grit their teeth, and stretch out their hand as far as possible. The hand mustn't be close to the body, because the teacher didn't want to come near the lice and smelly clothes of anyone who hadn't done his homework. The Arabic teacher would hold the ruler tight and hit the culprit on the back of the hand with all her strength, and she was very strong.

Almost all the teachers hit us. Some of them would walk through the class holding a hose. Others had a long thin bamboo cane. In the teachers' room there was a whip, and the teachers who were on yard duty would wave it as they watched over us in the yard during recess. The science teacher hit me with it once while I was taking a leak. He came into the toilets, which were filthy as usual, and whipped anyone who happened to be there. "Animals! Pigs!" he shouted. The whip stung, but it wasn't too bad.

I got fewer beatings than anyone else, fewer than the girls even. I always did my homework. I never made noise in class. I didn't talk with anyone. I spent recess at my desk with my hands folded. Some teachers favored the peer pressure system: If the class had been too noisy during recess, everyone who'd been there got a beating. Everyone except the ones whose parents taught at the school. They were exempt.

The *taftish* was the most frightening of all. The nurse would come in, in the middle of class, and each of us—knowing the routine—would take out our cotton handkerchief right away, spread it out in front of us, and place our palms on top of it. If you didn't have a handkerchief, you got hit. If you'd used it and it was dirty, you got hit. Anyone whose hands were dirty or whose fingernails were long got sent home. I always had a handkerchief. I had two, in fact—one that stayed clean for the *taftish* and one that I used.

The nurse would pick out a few kids at random and, with two thin sticks, she'd inspect their hair for lice. She'd always find some, and she'd scream and hit the culprit. Whichever teacher happened to be in charge of the class would help her. The two of them would write *I have lice* on a piece of paper, stick it on the foreheads of the ones who'd been checked, and send them home. "It's time your mother saw what she lets out of her house," was the nurse's standard line. They never found lice in my hair.

Everyone at school thought it was all right to hit. The janitor too. He'd come into the classroom, and pull out three kids. Two of them would carry the black plastic garbage pail and the third would gather up the remains of the sandwiches and wrappings and cans from the yard. If the janitor decided the yard still wasn't clean enough, you got hit. It happened to me once. One of the kids holding the garbage pail told the janitor I hadn't picked up all the litter. He gave me one slap, just one, because the janitor was our neighbor and he knew my father.

I got two whacks on the back of my hand with the wooden ruler from the music teacher because I didn't recognize one song he played on his oud. Once I got hit because the garbage pail in class was dirty, and it was my day to be garbage pail monitor. I got whipped across the back by the vice principal because I'd been afraid to climb onto the roof on Independence Day to stick the flag in a barrel of sand above the teachers' room. There were no stairs.

The only one who didn't hit us was the agriculture teacher. He was all right, died of a heart attack not long ago. He was the only teacher who came to school in a suit and tie, the only teacher who owned a car: a blue Subaru. He parked it far away from the tractors of the other teachers, which they'd use directly after school to go out to their strawberry fields. In agriculture class we cleaned the teacher's car. We loved his car, and he was always pleased. When we finished, he'd throw us the ball. We loved to play soccer.

My Only Friend in
Tira Was Hospitalized

My only friend in Tira was hospitalized. We were in the eighth grade. He was the only kid who was willing to sit next to me in class without the teacher making him.

One day he didn't come to school. On my way home, I knocked on his door, but nobody answered. His uncle in the neighborhood grocery store said he was sick. He had a headache, and they'd taken him to the hospital in Ramatayim. My parents dressed up. My mother bought a bag of snack bars and wrapped them the way you wrap a gift, and we drove off to visit him.

It was my first visit in Ramatayim and the first time I'd seen a hospital. It had an enormous gate and two heavy doors at the entrance that you couldn't open unless you were a doctor and knew the code. His parents looked sadder than usual. He was an only child. My father said his mother had such a nice ass he couldn't understand why they had just the one.

No one was allowed in to visit him except me. My friend looked the same as always. He said that sometimes his head hurt and he would hear strange things. I didn't pay any attention. He looked fine to me, didn't even have a fever. Next to the other bed in the room there was a kid who was holding a broom and pretending to shoot. He was a little older than us, and he liked to play war. My friend said that whenever they played together, the kid kept saying, "He's an Iraqi, he's an Iraqi."

My friend's parents had bought him a computer game with cars, and he let me play with it. My parents would never buy me such an expensive game. I always envied him. He never ate Popsicles, only fancy ice cream bars. He had a bike and nice clothes, a watch with a calculator, and an Atari. My mother said it was because he was an only child. She couldn't afford fancy ice cream bars for all four of us.

He was the only one of my friends who didn't get on my mother's nerves when he came to visit. She claimed the other parents sent their kids over to our house just to get rid of them, and she asked me not to let them in, but when it came to him she was always nice and even invited him to join us for a meal. He usually declined.

Father kept saying he couldn't understand why they didn't have another kid. They had plenty of money, after all. And what if something happened to that kid? My friend's father owned an enormous tractor with a windshield and an air-conditioned cab, and my father said he plowed every field in Tel Mond, working from dawn till dusk, and wouldn't pass up a single job. They had a new car, and it always stood right outside their home, covered by a white tarpaulin. They hardly ever used it, it was just for appearances, my father said. They never went out. My friend's father only used the tractor, because on Fridays and Saturdays when he wasn't working for the Jews he'd be plowing the fields in Tira.

Suddenly, in the middle of the game, my friend went berserk. He started screeching "Laaaaa! Laaaaa!" and in no time at all lots of male nurses showed up, took me out of the room, and tied my friend to the bed. It was scary. I'd never seen anything like it. I asked my parents what had happened, and they said we had to go home.

We didn't talk at all on our way back to Tira. Father drove in silence, with Mother beside him and me in the back, as usual. My parents wouldn't let me sleep with my grandmother anymore by then, but that night they pretended not to notice when I sneaked into her bed. They told her what had happened at the hospital.

"They shouldn't have taken you," she said, and hugged me tight. "Don't cry. God will cure him, he'll be back at school, you'll see. Go to sleep. Don't be scared, *ya habibi, yamma.*"

Parliament

Things seemed to be booming in those days. In my final year at grade school, they paved the road to Tira and hooked us up to the phone system, the soccer team moved up a league, they opened a swimming pool, and someone in Taiyiba connected the houses to cable TV.

Every single house in the village was hooked up. Nobody watched anything else, only closed-circuit cable. Everyone simply loved to watch people they knew appearing on TV. They saw them in the grocery store commercials that were shown between Indian or Egyptian films.

During Ramadan of that year, which took place in summer, they decided to hold a quiz show on cable, with prizes. Everyone in the village was allowed to take part. Within two days the quiz became a battle of honor, and every family in the village took it seriously. Some families would gather every day, to count how many of them had succeeded in giving the right answers and to prepare for the following day. The elections were coming up, and the competition between families was at an all-time high. Every family was hoping to strengthen its position in the village through the quiz show. Our family was one of the oldest in the village, but it was very small, and my father knew full well that we didn't stand a chance in the elections. By the time the quiz show was over, Father knew whom to vote for.

Father didn't miss a single screening of the quiz show on cable. The questions were very easy at first, like "When was the Prophet Mohammed born?" and Father would answer right away. His lips would mouth the quizmaster's text. Obviously, he had no intention of phoning in himself or of taking part with all those idiots who got caught up in their silly games. But the truth was that Father wasn't a hundred percent sure of himself, and he'd always wait to hear whether his answer had been confirmed by the quizmaster after some other listener had phoned in.

One day, the people on cable decided to ask some tough questions, the really tricky kind, with complicated clues. It was the middle of Ramadan month by then, and the struggle over the cable quiz had completely taken over life in the village. It was the only thing people talked about. Some said the quizmaster would only take calls from his own relatives and demanded a panel of judges with representatives of all the families in the village to supervise the competition while it was being aired.

That's when the toughest question of all was presented. It had been written by the school principal, who was the quizmaster's father. The larger families got their act together and started sending representatives to the cable station—huge guys who could beat the hell of out of you—to observe things from up close. This ritual show of strength gained momentum, to the point where there were so many representatives you could hardly see or hear the quizmaster asking the questions.

People got into squabbles on the air or shoved each other, and every now and then someone would let out a salvo of curses that could be heard in every home in the village. The cable people realized it was time to do something, and they moved the quiz to the soccer field. The only ones who watched from home were the deep thinkers and speed-dialers in each household. All the others took their places in the field as soon as the fast was over for the day. People swarmed through the streets toward the soccer field, almost running, before they'd had a chance to digest their hurried post-fast meal.

Father hadn't taken any part in the game up until then. He and the principal had been in the same class, and he always used to tell us how the principal had been a nobody when it came to schoolwork and had gone to some second-rate teachers college. His grades—Father's, that is—were the best in his class, and if he'd had enough money to finish university he would have become a doctor long ago.

The day the competition moved to the stadium was when they announced the Big Question. When my father heard that the principal, his classmate, had composed the hardest question, he stood up and plodded heavily toward the TV. "Get me a pen," he commanded. "Now, be quiet." And when the quizmaster repeated the question, Father wrote it on his palm:

From the land of Uncle Sam. Blue as the sky. Brings nothing but trouble. Can begin with two letters. And Abd el-Wahab lives there.

It was his battle now. Our family may have been small, but we saw ourselves as being very smart. My father copied the question from his palm to his notebooks and studied each and every word. "Has anyone solved it yet?" he asked.

"No, not yet, Father."

Time passed, and nobody seemed any closer to an answer. Father got angry and said the question was actually very dumb and he couldn't think like those idiots anyway. The program continued until the meal that marks the beginning of the fast, at about 5 A.M. Father stayed up and continued to ponder the question. Nobody found the answer that day, and on the following day people started to say that the principal had deliberately composed a question that had no answer. He represented his own family in the municipal elections, after all, and he'd do anything to undermine the others.

In the morning, Father phoned in and asked for time off from work until *'id el-fitr*—in other words, until the competition was over. Then he sat down with all the encyclopedias we had in the house and started digging. He checked even the unlikeliest meanings of the words. There were rumors about people who'd found the solution. There were dozens of phone calls and dozens of answers, but nobody had come up with the right one. Then my father began looking for religious connotations in the question. From time to time he thought he might be on to something, and he'd yell the answer to us, to make sure we gave him the credit if anyone phoned in meanwhile with the same answer.

A few days went by, and my father had to strike out all the answers he'd thought of that had been suggested by other people and proved wrong. Then he decided to check out the ones that remained. He never would have phoned in. He wasn't sure enough of himself, so he decided to go ask the station manager if any of his answers was right. If it turned out one was, he would forfeit the prize and promise not to phone in until the competition was over. When father returned from his visit with the station manager, we could tell he'd failed.

There were only two days left until the holiday, and the answer had yet to be found. Heads of families began proposing ideas for the big prize to be awarded to the winner at a grand ceremony in the soccer field on the eve of 'id el-fitr.

That night, Father didn't set foot outside his room. A moment before the show began, he opened the door, walked over to me, and said, with trembling lips and teary eyes, "I'm out of cigarettes. Go buy me some."

On my way home, I looked down at the pack of cigarettes in my hand. Parliaments, Father's favorites. AMERICAN BLUE, it said on the wrapper, and there was a picture of a blue sky. Suddenly it all fell into place. "Father, it's Parliament," I told him. "I think the answer is Parliament."

Father looked at me, sat me down, and took his place beside me. He knew it was the right answer. He and the school principal smoked Parliament Longs. "Parliament is an American cigarette," I told him. "The pack is blue as the sky. Cigarettes cause nothing but trouble. You can write Parliament in Arabic either with a P or with a B. And Abd el-Wahab Darawsheh is a member of the Knesset, the Parliament."

Without saying a word, Father leaped to the phone and dialed the number. The principal could be seen on the screen, sitting on a blue sofa in the center of the stage. The quizmaster was sitting beside him, and behind them were some thugs whose job was to manage the incoming calls. The line was busy. Father was all worked up. He kept dialing, again and again. Then he rushed out of the house and ran to the soccer field. He had to get the chance to answer before the principal gave it away.

Fifteen minutes later I saw Father on TV, trying to get through the barrier of thugs who were blocking the entrance to the makeshift studio. Then a cameraman walked up to him, and I could hear him say, "I have the answer."

The principal heard him too. I could see him get up out of his stately seat, walk over to his son, and ask him to put Father on the air. "I want the whole village to see he didn't solve it," he said. The manager must have told him about Father's incorrect answers. The quizmaster signaled something to one of the thugs, and my father moved up onto the stage, barely able to catch his breath. He grabbed the microphone, walked up to the principal's seat, looked him in the eye, and said, "Parliament."

"Correct!" the principal's son shouted at once, but the principal got up and took the microphone from Father.

"There can be no solution without an explanation," he said.

Father took back the microphone. He knew now that victory was his. He turned toward the camera. "Parliament is a cigarette from the land of Uncle Sam. Cigarettes bring nothing but trouble. The pack is blue as the sky. You can spell it with a P or a B, and Abd el-Wahab Darawsheh is a member of Parliament." The crowd listened to the answer and realized it was correct. They didn't need any confirmation. Everyone cheered like crazy. Even the quizmaster, the principal's son, seemed happy to hear the answer that only he and his father had known. He encouraged the crowd.

"Congratulations," he said to Father. "You've won five kilos of ground meat from the Triangle Butcher Stop." But my father and the principal just went on staring at each other, panting.

The entire crowd was applauding by then, delighted that a member of a small family had figured it out. Father was still standing there with the microphone in his hand, staring at the defeated principal. The camera focused on him as he lifted the microphone again and said, with a winner's smile, "It's my son. My son solved it."

The Last Days

Those were the last days of ninth grade. Every morning I'd march to school feeling very proud. I knew people were looking at me now, but I didn't look back at them, didn't turn my head. I tried to stay focused on myself and to look like someone who is absorbed in deep thoughts, maybe pondering some question in physics.

They started treating me differently at school too. Until then, I'd been in the weakest of the ninth-grade classes, because my father had no connections. I was the best student in the class, but it was a class where half the kids couldn't read.

A few days after 'id el-fitr, the principal himself came to see us. He shook my hand and asked to speak with Father. He said the Jews were opening a new school for gifted students, and they wanted to test Arab students too. The principal said the list of candidates from Tira had already been submitted, but that after I solved the riddle he managed to persuade the Jews to let me take the test too. He said they take one out of a thousand and I stood a chance, but we mustn't be too disappointed if I didn't get in. "The tests are tough," he said.

The auditorium on the old Hebrew University campus was packed with Arab kids from all over the country. Tira alone had sent a whole busload. The wealthier parents had taken their kids by car. Everyone seemed really smart. I knew right away that I didn't have a chance.

A week later all the kids at school had received letters regretting to inform them that they hadn't passed the exam. I was the only one who didn't get a letter. I figured I'd been so inadequate they didn't even bother notifying me. They assumed I'd figure it out for myself.

When Father found out that everyone except me had received rejection letters, he was frantic. He started searching for their phone number—he talked to the principal, then called the regional superintendent—but nobody knew how to contact that school. Father said they'd pulled a fast one on us. There was no such school; the State of Israel just wanted to find out about the Arab school system.

A few days later—it was on a Friday—I was working in the olive grove behind the house with Father and my three brothers. Mother shouted through the kitchen window that there was a phone call in Hebrew. Father put down the bucket of olives and went running. He's a fast runner, my father, and I ran after him. He didn't even take off his shoes and wound up tracking mud all over the carpet. When I entered, he had just hung up. He clenched his two fists, raised his arms, and shouted, "Yes!" Then he hugged me, beaming with joy. "You're in!" he told me.

The following day, as we stood in rows for morning drills, the principal came over to congratulate me: *Mabruk,* he said, and ordered everyone to applaud. Everyone knew I'd been accepted.

There was this girl in school named Rim. Maybe now there was a chance she would love me the way I loved her, I thought. She must have known who I was by then, even though I'd never spoken to her. I used to seek her out and follow her around. I knew when she had recess, and when she finished school each day of the week, and how much time it took her to get from her classroom to the gate—so I could stall and take the same amount of time.

After two years I'd become an expert at following Rim home from a distance, far enough away not to be noticed but close enough for her to see me. She must have heard about the new school. Everyone was talking about it. Maybe she'd come with her parents to the party my father was throwing in honor of my having been accepted. They'd bought me a new outfit already. She'd be impressed, I thought. I even considered shaving my mustache a little, but I was afraid it would grow in black. Besides, only the lousiest students started shaving early.

My parents and hers had met on a bus trip to Egypt. They were in the same group, struck up a conversation, had their pictures taken together, and visited one another from time to time. I started seeking her out after I saw a picture of her near the pyramids. Pretty, with her head tilted slightly, long black hair, and mature eyes. All I knew about her was her name and that she was in the eighth grade. I'd met her parents a few times when they came over. Now the timing was right. Now I could talk to her. I was entitled. I was smart, and I was going away.

When she comes, I'll ask her to wait for me. She knows I love her. She's seen me following her. I'll promise her always to think of her and to return to her when I finish school. We'll be married and we'll be happy. When she finds out what I've done for her these past two years, when she sees the picture of her by the pyramids in my wallet, when she discovers that I know her schedule by heart, she's bound to agree to wait.

I walked behind her, feeling very proud, realizing people were observing me and that everyone was filled with admiration. If anyone makes fun of me today, of my mustache, of my bag—people will know that it's just because they're jealous, poor sports who can't accept defeat. Rim's flower-print pants fluttered in the wind, then clung to her legs. I lowered my gaze. It was the last day of school, and she was going to find out.

Mango

"Today you're the *aris,* the groom, the star," my father says, and goes to the door to greet our guests. In my neatly ironed cotton pants and my white shirt buttoned up to my neck, my hair not quite dry yet, and my tiny mustache, I take my place by his side. With us are all my aunts with their children and families.

Father's friends from work are the first to arrive. They shake my hand, saying *Mabruk* and Congratulations. They bring gifts, mostly cheap Parker pens. They say they hope I'll become a rocket scientist. They say I'll build the first Arab atom bomb. Then Rim's parents arrive, carrying a gift-wrapped box, and shake my hand. She must have been held up, I think. She's got to come today.

The grown-ups are drinking coffee, eating *knaffeh* and mango, and laughing from time to time. My brothers are with my cousins outside. They're playing hide-and-seek and they invite me to join them, but I say I don't want to get my clothes dirty. I sit on the fence separating the house from the street.

I want to go to bed. The guests leave, and my mother begins cleaning up the yard. My brothers have gone indoors.

Father comes out and asks me to go turn off the water in the mango grove behind the house.

It's dark out there, and I'm scared.

Father insists and doesn't understand why I'm scared. He gets annoyed and slaps me. I start crying and go to turn off the water.

When I come back inside, Grandma is shouting at Father. Mother is washing the dishes, and she says I ought to apologize. I enter the room. My younger brother is in his bed already, next to mine. I crawl into bed without taking my clothes off, pull the covers over my head, and let the tears roll down my cheeks.

Grandma comes in and mutters something I can't make out. She tries to pull down the blanket, but I cling to it. She raises her voice at my father. "You're killing the boy. Come see for yourself how he's trembling. You have no soul."

Grandma puts her hand on the blanket and tells me to calm down. She's crying too.

"It's best for you that you're going away," she says. "Thank God it's over."

PART THREE

I Wanted to Be a Jew

The Toughest Week
of My Life

I look more Israeli than the average Israeli. I'm always pleased when Jews tell me this. "You don't look like an Arab at all," they say. Some people claim it's a racist thing to say, but I've always taken it as a compliment, a sign of success. That's what I've always wanted to be, after all: a Jew. I've worked hard at it, and I've finally pulled it off.

There was one time when they picked up on the fact that I was an Arab and recognized me. So right after that I became an expert at assuming false identities. It was at the end of my first week of school in Jerusalem. I was on the bus going home to Tira. A soldier got on and told me to get off. I cried like crazy. I'd never felt so humiliated.

Sometimes, before I fall asleep, the familiar smell of the boarding school comes over me and paralyzes every muscle in my body. It belongs nowhere but there, and it comes back to haunt me: the smell of a different world, of buildings and furniture and carpets and people I never knew. A smell that used to make me feel uneasy, every single time. I spent three years there, and I never got used to it. That smell remained foreign to me.

The first week at the school was the toughest week of my life. Every day gave me new reasons to cry my heart out. I cried when I had to say good-bye to Grandma. "Just don't talk politics," she said, and kissed me.

Then Father drove me to the meeting place at the entrance to Jerusalem. The drive up the winding roads to Jerusalem scared me. What if Father didn't make it back in one piece? It was raining hard, and a long row of cars was inching its way up the mountain. I prayed in silence that I'd miss the school bus and would have to go back home.

There was a row of tables where people gave each of us a name tag to hang around our necks. They misspelled my name. They gave us envelopes with a piece of paper that told us the color of our building and our room number. It took me a while to find the place. My three roommates had gotten there first and had left me the bed farthest from the window, closest to the door. Everyone said Hi, and one of them shook my hand and read the name on my name tag. I didn't correct him.

That first week, I didn't know what to do with my tray in the dining room. I didn't know how to eat with a knife and fork. I didn't know the Jews put the gravy on top of their rice, instead of putting it in a separate bowl. I cried when my roommates found out I'd never heard of the Beatles and laughed at me. They laughed when I said *bob* music instead of *pop* music. They laughed when I threatened to complain to Principal Binhas—instead of Pinhas. "What did you say his name was?" they asked, and like an idiot I repeated it: "Binhas." They laughed at the pink sheets Mother had bought me specially.

They laughed at my pants. At first, I even believed them when they said they really wanted to know where they could buy such pants. "Do they make special pants for Arabs?" they asked.

After English class, one of the students said I had the same accent as Arafat. As far as I knew, Arafat was the guy from the *Aden Hafla* cassette. Another kid said I looked like the blind kanoon player on TV. All through the first week, they kept calling me Abu Jamil el-Anzeh, the guy in the Arabic course on Educational TV.

That first week I also met Adel, the Arab who was a year ahead of me. I saw him in the dining room and recognized him at once. He was at a table with the girls, and he was eating his chicken with his fingers. I knew I didn't want to look like him, but just seeing him there kept me going. Within two days, we'd moved in together. I had no problem persuading one of his roommates to swap with me.

Adel thought my sheets were really nice. He came from a village in the Upper Galilee, four hours away by bus. They'd made a film about him once for Israel TV. Showed him dribbling on the basketball court, to prove that Arabs and Jews can live together. Pinhas said about him in the film, "Adel brought his whole village on his back," and Adel said it was a compliment. He was a good student and didn't need to study much. He answered in class and wasn't shy.

That first week I had to read more pages in Hebrew than I'd read in Tira all the way through to the ninth grade. I gave up and didn't do anything. They also had a placement test in physics. Adel got a hundred, and I couldn't answer a single question. One week was enough. It was obvious that I was going home for good.

When I tell my family what I've been through this week, they'll never send me back, I thought. They'll understand me. They'll realize it's a different world, and I can't live there. I'll tell them how out of place I felt during the Rosh Hashanah meal, how I don't know a single word of their songs. I'll tell them how I cry myself to sleep each night. And how I can't stop thinking about my family, because I worry that something bad will happen to them: that Grandma will die or Father will have a car accident. I'll tell them there are some bad kids at the school, with earrings, and the girls walk around in shorts. I'll explain it has been the hardest week of my life, and they'll let me stay home.

Polanski

When it was time to go home for the Rosh Hashanah break, I packed everything I'd brought with me and got on the bus. It was my first trip alone on a public bus, and if I hadn't followed some of the kids who'd gotten on before me, I would never have known you have to pay the driver right at the beginning.

Adel and I took our seats on one bench. There was no one on the bench across from us, and Adel said maybe the girls from the our school would sit there, but it didn't happen. All the kids from our school sat down in front, carrying on and making a hell of a racket.

I was petrified of the trip, afraid I wouldn't make it home or that I'd get off at the wrong stop and be lost. My father had written it all down for me in a notebook:

Take the bus to the central bus station, get off with everyone else. Then he wrote: *Bus 947, Haifa local, get off at the Kfar Sava stop. Walk as far as Meir hospital, then look for the Tira taxi stand. Take taxi to Tira.*

Adel was supposed to go to his village, Nahf, which is a much longer journey. You go as far as Haifa, then take another bus to Karmi'el, and there you can spend hours waiting for a bus that goes by his village. He said he'd probably walk from Karmi'el. "It's not that far, just half an hour's walk."

Adel didn't want to go home. He was disappointed to have to leave after just one week. He asked the principal if he could spend the holiday break at school, but Pinhas said that was impossible. I invited him to Tira, and he accepted. I was glad to have someone to help me find the way, and he was glad to save time and money. He asked if we had any pretty girls in our neighborhood.

The bus leaves from the front gate of the school, and its first stop is just a few minutes away, at the Polanski Vocational School. The students there look different from the ones at our school, and Adel and I don't look like any of them. The bus is full of students now, shouting and swearing, and girls in black high-heeled shoes and big earrings who spend the whole bus ride putting on makeup.

Three kids crowd into the seat facing Adel and me, and two others stand next to them, holding on to the metal bars. I feel stifled, dead. I tell Adel I'm getting off at the next stop. "Don't be a retard." he says. "I'm not going to pay for another ticket to the central bus station."

I'm already sorry I invited him, sorry I ever met him, sorry

I got on the bus with him. I can tell we're in trouble, and within minutes my fears prove true.

One of the kids on the bench across from us asks Adel where he's from.

"Nahf," Adel says.

The kids laugh and turn to me. "And you?"

I put on the biggest grin I can muster, trying to be the most polite person in the world. They're not going to hurt me. I was in Seeds of Peace. I know Jews. They've got to leave me alone. "From Tira," I say. "It's near Kfar Sava." I try to keep up the smile, even though they're already laughing at me. Quickly I whisper to Adel, "Let's get off, I'll pay for your ticket." But he won't do it. One thing's for sure: I'm never getting on this bus again.

The kids across from us are whispering, laughing, repeating the names of our villages and deliberately mispronouncing them. They're laughing at our names, and we don't do anything about it. To take part in the general hilarity would be ridiculous, so I keep quiet. They start singing something that sounds familiar, but instead of "The Jew is dead"—the way we sing it—they sing "Mohammed is dead." They sing loudly, and some of their classmates join in. I press the STOP button. The hell with Adel. I'm getting off. I pick up my bag, controlling myself, holding back my tears.

Once I get off, Adel decides to get off too. I see him only after I'm on the sidewalk. One of the students opens a window and spits. He misses us.

Adel starts shouting at me. "I can't believe it! Do you even know where we are? Do you have any idea what bus we need to take now? Why do you think the same thing won't happen on the next bus we take?"

I was willing to risk being lost. I was just so relieved it was over. My father had given me enough money. We took a cab back to the central bus station. All I wanted was for the Polanski kids not to get on our bus to Kfar Sava.

Ben Gurion

There was nothing in my father's explanations about Ben Gurion Airport. The sonofabitch lied to me. How I hated him then. When the bus stopped for the first time, I was sure we'd reached Kfar Sava, but it was the roadblock at the entrance to Ben Gurion Airport.

A soldier got on and told Adel and me to get off. Then he asked us for our IDs.

"We're not sixteen yet," Adel told him, and answered all his questions: where we're from, where we're going, where we study.

The soldier asked us to open our bags, and the bus went into the airport without us. The soldier searched through our books, our sheets, and our clothes and said we should wait for the bus to return and pick us up on the way out of the airport.

I'm not getting back on that bus, I decided. I'm not willing to be stared at like I-don't-know-what. I've had it. I can't take this anymore. I'd survived the roommates, the dining room, and the Polanski kids, but this was the last straw. I cried like a baby. I broke down. Even the soldier felt uneasy. He said it was just routine. He brought me some water. "What's the matter?" he asked.

I didn't drink it. I phoned my father at home. I could barely blurt out the words.

My father screamed, "Calm down, what happened?" He was upset.

"Come here and get me right away," I shouted, to make sure he understood I wasn't coming home on my own. "I'm at the airport."

Adel preferred to keep quiet. He said he could have been in Nahf already and he was sorry he'd joined me.

I sat there crying, waiting for my father.

"What happened?" my father asked, when he finally arrived to pick us up. I didn't answer. I sat in front and Adel sat in back. My face was all swollen, and Adel told him that a soldier had taken us off the bus and I wouldn't get back on. Father said, "Are you crazy? What's got into you? Is that something to cry about?"

"I told him a million times, but he wouldn't listen," Adel said.

I didn't say a word.

Adel and my father talked about school, about the food they gave us there, and about what they called "four o'clock snack," which was cake and juice. Adel said they serve meat for dinner every day. They talked about the big library and the playground. My father said a million kids would like to be in my place, and there I was, crying like a baby. "Do you want to come back to Tira, to study with all the bums, is that what you want? Fine, suit yourself. But don't come complaining to me later if everyone says they threw you out of school after a single week. Do you want people to say you flunked, that you couldn't make it at a good school? Have you thought about how people will look at you?"

My tears hadn't dried yet, but I could tell right away that my father wasn't about to let me stay home. I had no choice. I'd have to go back to the school.

"Look at Adel," my father said. "Why isn't he crying?" Then he laughed at me. The sonofabitch knew they took Arabs off the bus at the airport. He'd taken the same bus when he went to the university. "Nobody ever told me to get off," he said. "They didn't notice I was an Arab. Every time the soldiers told an Arab to get off, I'd get up and shout, 'Take me off too, I'm an Arab!' and I'd hold up my ID card and wave it proudly. What's the matter with you? What a jellyfish you are. Some soldier jerk can make you behave like this? Just look at yourself."

I took that bus line hundreds of times after that. Each time, I'd feel the fear again. It didn't let up until we'd passed the airport. The only time they ever made me get off was on that first trip. After that, they didn't notice me anymore. I felt sorry for the Arabs who were taken off, and I thanked God they hadn't picked on me.

In my second week at the school, I shaved off my mustache. I told Adel we had to learn to pronounce the letter *p* properly. He didn't care. The Bible teacher gave me a tip: "Hold a piece of paper up to your mouth. If the paper moves, you've said a *p*," he said. Adel laughed at me, and when the paper moved, he said he couldn't tell the difference. He was convinced there was really no difference between *b* and *p*, that it was all in my head, and that Hebrew is a screwed-up language. He didn't see why they had to have two different letters for the same sound.

In my second week at school I bought myself some pants in a Jewish store. I bought a Walkman and some tapes in Hebrew. After that, I'd always have my Walkman and a book in Hebrew whenever I went through the airport. I didn't come across the Polanski kids anymore. They were liable to recognize me. I took a cab whenever I needed to get to or from the central bus station. Adel and I stayed friends, but I never invited him home again.

Shorts

At school, I got to play with real guns. I knew how to use a carbine and an Uzi: snap the magazine in, cock the weapon, hold the gun to my shoulder, position myself like a sniper, and shoot. On school trips, the teachers would have weapons, and I soon became the student in charge. The weapons were heavy, and I was the only student who was prepared to carry them. I felt proud to be walking around with a gun across my shoulder.

Our history teacher was a left-winger. He always let me have his gun and asked me to walk close to him, because someone once made a comment about it, and he explained to me that it was his responsibility. He wouldn't let me carry the magazines, even though he could have trusted me blindly.

Pretty soon I started sitting at the back of the bus with the other kids and singing their favorite bus-trip songs. I started taking the lead, and they'd join in the refrain. I knew the words by heart. When I was in elementary school, we had one favorite song that we'd chant over and over again—"*Dos, dos ya chauffeur, al 199*"—a song that urges the driver to go faster, 199 kilometers an hour. "Don't worry about the cops. We're the children of Palestine. Palestine is our country, and the Jew is our dog, knocking on our door like a beggar." We sang without understanding a word. Once, our history teacher in Tira asked if anyone in the class knew what Palestine was, and nobody did, including me. Then he asked contemptuously if any of us had ever seen a Palestinian, and Mohammed the Fatso, who was afraid of having his knuckles rapped, said he'd once been driving with his father in the dark and they'd seen two Palestinians. That day, the history teacher rapped every single one of us on the knuckles, launching his attack with Mohammed the Fatso. He whacked us with his ruler, ranting, "We are Palestinians, you are Palestinians, I'm a Palestinian! You nincompoops, you animals, I'll teach you who you are!"

On our class trips, whenever we slept outdoors we'd light a fire, and some kids would play the guitar. Nobody in Tira had ever played a guitar. We sang Beatles hits, and Israeli rock band songs too. Mashina, for instance. I knew already who they were, and I forced myself to learn their songs. I couldn't stand that music at first, but within a few months it grew on me and I started liking it. Whenever I'd go home on vacation I'd scream at my brothers, who still listened to Fairuz and Abed el-Halim. When my father took me to the bus stop in Kfar Sava, I'd beg him to switch to a Hebrew radio station or at least to lower the volume. It wasn't that I was ashamed. I really couldn't stand them anymore. I told him my ear had grown used to other things.

On the trip to Wadi Qilt, I was carrying an Uzi and walked with the first group of hikers, with the teachers and the guides. Suddenly we heard something. The guide held up his hand and told all the kids to stand behind him. The history teacher yanked the gun off my shoulder, and I fell and hit my elbow. The teacher snapped in the magazine and cocked the weapon. And then we saw it was another group of schoolchildren.

It was my old class from Tira. I recognized them and they recognized me. They had a new teacher, one I'd never seen before. He asked his students to stand to the side to let us pass, because the passage was too narrow. I held my bleeding arm, lowered my gaze, and focused on my elbow.

The kids from Tira called out my name, and I pretended not to hear them. "Hey, look, it's him. Over there, in the shorts," they said. I passed by them quickly. A few of them said, "Hi, how're you doing?" and I wanted to dig a hole and hide. I nodded and kept going. Later, when some of the kids asked me if I knew them, I said I didn't. "But they knew your name," one of them insisted, and I said it was a common name among Arabs.

Once an Arab,
Always an Arab

My father says, Once an Arab, always an Arab. And he's got a point. He says the Jews can give you the feeling that you're one of them, and you can really like them and think they're the nicest people you've ever known, but sooner or later you realize you don't stand a chance. For them you'll always be an Arab.

Sometimes when I'm at home, I steal a few of my father's books. I hate reading Arabic, but I owe it to myself to look at those books. To understand why Mahmoud Darwish is considered great, and why Emil Habibi was awarded the Israel Prize. The last book I stole was *Hamarat al-Balad* by Salman Natour. This young Arab—a poet, maybe, or an author—writes about life in a Tel Aviv pub. He describes all the left-wing Jews, who are really very nice to him. They listen to him with great interest and introduce him to new friends. Pretty young girls sit beside him and sometimes even kiss him. He recalls how at one stage he thought he could blend in completely. I feel like an idiot for ever thinking I could blend in too.

My father used to say I'd be the first Arab to build an atom bomb. He really believed it. Adel says no way. He used to think so too, but even if he were the smartest person in the world, they'd never let him study that kind of thing. There are some things an Arab can never become. The two of us were sitting in the guard's room. We were alarm monitors that night. Every night since the Gulf War started two students had to stay up and wake the others if the alarm went off. Adel said he wanted to be the one to wake the girls because there were bound to be a few who slept in their underwear. The thought appealed to me, but I laughed at him anyway. In the drawer under his bed he had some girlie magazines. Sometimes, when there was nobody around, I'd lock the door and look through them, and all that time I'd think to myself, The guy's a pervert.

The war was drawing to an end. There hadn't been any alarms for several nights in a row, and Adel said there was still hope and the Iraqis might win. They were just waiting for the Americans to come closer. The Iraqis had enough oil to set the whole gulf on fire. All the aircraft carriers would be burned. The problem was that they didn't have people who could think straight. If he'd been there, he'd have taught them how to win a war.

The uniformed guard in the glass booth across from us scared me. People in uniform always scared me. As far as I was concerned, all of them were police. I think he was a little scared of us too. Didn't say a word, just sat there with a book in his hand as if he were trying to do his homework. Every now and then he'd peek at us, and as soon as he made eye contact he'd turn back to his book. I thought he was a student, but Adel said he must be making up some matriculation exams and looked like someone who'd never make it.

Just don't let the alarm go off now. My parents have stopped wearing their gas masks, let alone staying in a sealed room. Mother told me that my father and brothers would go outdoors to see if there were any missiles in the air. They weren't the only ones. Nobody in the village stayed indoors. People went out, to make sure the Patriot missiles weren't working. Our neighbor started shouting for the missiles to come. It was as if he were trying to guide them past the Patriots. "Nooooo. . . . left . . . that's right. Yeah!" His children applauded, and the women went *lululu* the way they did at weddings.

The Arab newspapers wrote a story about a goat that could say "Sadaaaaaam." Then people began seeing Saddam's face in the moon. When I came home, my father couldn't believe I didn't see it myself. He took me outdoors and tried for hours to explain where I should look: where the nose was, where the mouth was, where the mustache was, and the beret. In the end, I did see him. It really did look like him. Not just like him— it *was* him. Look straight up.

Matzohs

When we were little, we used to fight over matzohs. They were like trick-or-treat candies that you can only get for a few weeks and then they disappear. The women didn't need to bake during matzoh season. Everyone ate matzohs. With hummus, with salami, with beans, it was delicious. Grandma said the Jews kidnapped Dr. Jihad once, when he was still a little boy. His mother, a widow like my grandmother, cried all day. She looked for him all over Kfar Sava. She'd gone into a store to buy him an ice-cream bar, and he'd disappeared. Some men from the village joined her in the search. He was an only son, like my father. She almost died of grief, the poor woman. But eventually she found him. He was with some religious Jews, some rabbis, and they felt sorry for her and gave her back the child. They'd wanted to take some of his blood to put in their matzohs, my grandmother told us, but we didn't believe that Dr. Jihad was ever little.

Sagi was the first boy to invite me to his home for the Passover seder. I had just started shaving my beard. They had a small apartment but a nice one, in a building with an elevator. There were no elevators in our village. The only ones we saw were at

Meir hospital in Kfar Sava. He said I had nothing to worry about, that his parents were left-wingers. His mother was from South America and had been in the revolution. She was an ardent socialist. His father was from Poland, and I just had to see his pictures from when he was doing computer studies in the U.S. That was in the sixties, and he dressed like a flower child. There was a younger sister too, who played the piano in the living room, and in the kitchen they had a small television set on a swivel. They were nice to me. His mother kept smiling, good-natured. She cooked all day long. When she asked Sagi to bring some chairs from the neighbor, I helped him.

We weren't close friends. Sometimes I'd borrow cassettes from him, because he liked hard rock and I wanted to learn what it sounded like. I didn't particularly like the music, but he'd invited me, so I went. I had a hard time going home in those days. At some point in my adolescence it dawned on me that my parents hadn't been treating me right.

Later that evening, an old man arrived, and another family with kids, including a girl our age. We sat to the side, and they sang. The girl held the Passover book and looked at the pictures and spoke a different language. She knew some of the songs, and sang them in a foreign accent, and seemed happy. She had just arrived in the country. A pretty girl.

That's when I learned about Jewish holidays. You sit around a table, you dress up, you have wine, you don't roast anything on a spit. And even if there are a lot of people, you don't use disposable dishes. There's no hummus on the table. You eat chopped liver and all sorts of strange foods. They were nice to me and didn't put everything on my plate. They kept saying, "You don't have to if you don't like it." But I ate it. If it's good enough for them, it's good enough for me.

Sagi taught me lots of things. About the Haggadah, and the afikomen, and the ten plagues of Egypt, and who Elijah the Prophet was. He dressed up as Elijah, and I kept looking at the girl, but it's difficult to impress a girl when you don't speak her language. She lived in an *ulpan*, where she was studying Hebrew. She'd just arrived in the country, and she'd come to stay. She said, "It's a wonderful country," and I had no idea what she was talking about. Just you wait, I thought. Just you wait till you see the Polanski kids. Just you wait till you have to take the bus. But she really was happy. Her parents had stayed in Argentina, but it didn't matter to her, she said. She loved Eretz Yisrael.

We were sitting in Sagi's room. I didn't catch her name, and she didn't catch mine. Sagi knew a little Spanish, and he translated what she said. "Ask her if there are any Arabs where she studies," I said, and she said there weren't any. "She says she's heard about Arabs and she's not afraid of them at all," Sagi translated. And then he told her that there were Arabs at his school and that they were cool. She said she couldn't understand how we even agreed to study there, and that in her opinion, there was no such thing as a good Arab. Sagi thought that was funny. He told me she was a stupid thick-headed jerk, a real cow. He grabbed his head, pointed at me, and said, "He's an Arab." She laughed and said it wasn't nice to say such a thing about me.

The Happiest
Independence Day
of My Life

The teachers at my new school don't hit the students. There's no lice inspection. The teachers don't check your homework. You don't have to say "sir," and when you need to go to the bathroom you don't have to get permission; you can go whenever you want. And the bathrooms are clean and spacious, with a dryer that gives off hot air to dry your hands. I can't stand the dryer, but there are paper towels too. There are lots of cleaning people in blue uniforms. They're not allowed to hit. They don't even talk to the students.

You don't have to line up to go into class. You don't have to read the Koran every morning. You don't have one girl playing the same silly tune on the organ, and boys are allowed to sit next to girls.

Naomi sat next to me once, and I fell in love. I sank. I crashed. I'd put my head on my pillow, open my eyes, stare at the ceiling—and feel different. An unfamiliar feeling, a new kind of pain. In the dining room, in the library, in class, in the lobby, everywhere, my ears were pricked to hear her footsteps. I recognized them, every time. I recognized the sound from a distance: when she was barefoot, when she was in those black sandals, when she was in running shoes.

We hung out a lot together. Once we studied chemistry in her room. I sat on her bed, with the pretty sheets and the quilt. Her hair was long. Not black, not yellow, something in between. White hands. Freckled face. I loved those freckles. When she had kitchen duty, I helped her. In our class play at the end of tenth grade, I danced with her. In our first month in eleventh grade I told her I loved her. A week later she had a boyfriend.

I saw them hug each other in the snow. It was the first snow I'd ever seen. Quiet, lighting up the night, not banging on the windowpane like rain. I stood at the window, looking out at the lawn, which was covered in whiteness. After that, I spent most of my time just lying on my bed with my mouth open and my head aching, until they broke up.

On Holocaust Remembrance Day, Naomi wore a white blouse and read out of a black looseleaf about a little girl who sees her father on fire in the forest. At the end of the ceremony I told her I loved her, and she smiled. On Memorial Day for the Fallen Soldiers, she was furious because I hadn't stood at attention during the memorial siren. We were sitting together in biology class. Everyone else got up, and I stayed seated. I had lost a grandfather and an uncle in the war, after all. After the siren she didn't sit down. She took her bag and left.

She didn't show up for lunch. She wasn't in her room or in the library. What an idiot I was. What was the matter with me? Couldn't I have stood? Her father was killed in active duty after all. He died when she was still very little. There's a picture of him over her bed, with her on his shoulders. She must have been about three; she hardly remembers him. He was an officer in the IDF, and he'd been in charge of the evacuation of Yamit. He didn't die in the war. He'd had an accident on his way home from his base. The IDF took her on a trip to Canada once. They pay her tuition.

I sat at the school gate listening to sad music on my Walkman—the Cranes, maybe, or the Swans—and I waited for her.

Naomi got out of her mother's Mitsubishi. She had tears in her eyes. It was the first time I saw her mother. She looked at me and drove off. They'd been to the ceremony at the military cemetery on Mount Herzl. But that wasn't why she was sad.

"Why didn't you stand for the siren?"

I'm not Jewish.

"I love you. I've loved you for a long time. I told my mother that I love you. I cried, and I told her I couldn't take it anymore. Every time you told me *I love you* I thought, in my heart, *So do I, so do I.*" She smiled.

Now I understood what true joy was. I carried her bag to her room. I was ecstatic. It was the happiest Independence Day eve of my life.

A National Home

Sometimes I think about when I was young, and I thank God I'm not there anymore. What a mess I was: the way I looked, the way I felt. I'm so happy to be an adult. In the middle of twelfth grade I went to a café for the first time. It was one of those Tuesday evenings when they gave us time off. That's when I learned that you could order a salad as a separate course, served in a big bowl, and that there were different kinds. Salad on its own, without a *pitta*. We were sitting in Atara Café, where Amos Oz sat in *My Michael*. Naomi ordered a Greek salad, and I ordered a hot chocolate. Something familiar, something I could afford.

In twelfth grade, Naomi took me to the movies for the first time. I couldn't believe that girls could go into a movie theater. There used to be a movie theater in Tira, but not anymore. There's a small room, with walls of unpainted bricks and a television set. When we were little, Aunt Ibtissam's son, who was really big then, took us to see *Tarzan*. There were wooden chairs, like in elementary school. It was nothing more than a dark hovel. My little brother threw up right at the beginning, and all of us got out of there pretty fast. Everyone kept shouting and smoking, and when Tarzan's guys appeared in the forest there were catcalls and whistling. I was petrified.

I was frightened in twelfth grade too. The movie theater was bound to be full of people like the Polanski students. They'd recognize me and I'd have nowhere to run. Sometimes the Polanski kids would come to the school gate and scream, "Death to the Arabs!" I never went out into the yard beyond the fence. It seemed too risky, too far from the guard.

Naomi said I had nothing to be afraid of at the movies. We were going to see *Life According to Agfa,* and she said it was a movie the thugs would never go to, a movie for left-wingers like her. We could sit through the whole movie holding hands. I didn't have to be afraid of anyone.

The new life was exciting. I realized it wasn't only bad kids who went to the movies. Grown-ups went too. Men and women sat together. Everything was clean and neat. The chairs were padded, and everyone dressed nicely. Boy, was I glad to see the two Arab kitchen workers in the film. They were cool, actually, and funny. The thugs were the bad guys. I couldn't get over the pianist in the restaurant. Naomi said it was Danny Litani, a well-known singer. She didn't have a tape of his in her room, but she had one of some guy who sang "Things Have Got to Change," and "Just Get Out of the Territories." I couldn't believe a Jew would sing stuff like that.

Naomi was in a party called Ratz. She had a green shirt with the party logo, and she talked a lot about human beings as human beings. About how there was no difference between national groups, how individuals should be judged on their own merits, and how you shouldn't look at a whole group as if everyone were the same. She said that in every nation there are good people and bad people. I never really understood what she was talking about, but I took the whole thing seriously.

In twelfth grade I understood for the first time what '48 was. That it's called the War of Independence. In twelfth grade I understood that a Zionist was what we called a Sahyuni, and it wasn't a swearword. I knew the word. That's how we used to curse one another. I'd been sure that a Sahyuni was a kind of fat guy, like a bear. Suddenly I understood that Zionism is an ideology. In civics lessons and Jewish history classes, I started to understand that my aunt from Tulkarm is called a refugee, that the Arabs in Israel are called a minority. In twelfth grade I understood that the problem was serious. I understood what a national homeland was, what anti-Semitism was. I heard for the first time about "two thousand years of exile" and how the Jews had fought against the Arabs and the British. I didn't believe it. No way. The English had wanted the Jews here, after all. In Bible class, I discovered that Abraham was Isaac's father. In twelfth grade I discovered that it was Isaac, not Ismael, who'd been replaced with a sheep.

In twelfth grade, the kids in my class started running in the parking lot, getting into shape for the army. They were taken to all sorts of installations and training camps, and I received a bus pass and a ticket to the Israel Museum. Sometimes soldiers in uniform came to our school to talk with the students, and I wasn't allowed to take part. Our teacher always apologized. He was embarrassed to have to tell me it wasn't for me. In twelfth grade I understood I wouldn't be a pilot even if I wanted to be, not only because I wasn't fit and my grades weren't good enough. There was no way they would even call me up for the screening tests. I sure had a good laugh at my father.

An Educational Approach

That day, Mother and Father stayed home from work. They dressed up, and an hour and a half before the appointment they got in the car. They knew they mustn't be late. They had to look like parents. The night before, they'd come to pick me up at the hospital. The school guidance counselor had taken me to the Emergency Room at Shaarei Tsedek hospital. How I screamed at her when I heard she'd asked my parents to come! I'd shamed them in the worst way. And I'd shamed myself too. Now I'd hate myself even more.

I just kept praying: Don't let my parents find out. Don't let my father find out. But now they knew. They came to the hospital and saw me having my stomach pumped. They talked with the guidance counselor and took me back home to the village. My father's friend Bassem was with us. He and my father had been playing chess when the counselor called, and he offered to go along to see how I was doing.

Now I remember how this Bassem stood over my bed at the hospital and asked, "What's wrong with him? What's wrong with him?" And Father answered, "It's all because of that bitch of his, the Jewish whore."

I'd been tired and dizzy all the time. I could hardly fall asleep. I didn't sleep more than two hours a night, and I was having strong headaches. This had been going on for a few months. I couldn't concentrate, I couldn't think or sleep or even simply sit still. There was a strange buzzing in my ears, and it wouldn't stop. Headache pills never helped me, and the CAT scan didn't show a thing. The neurological tests were normal too.

One weekend when I had gone home, Mother took me to Amneh, our neighbor, Grandma's friend. She said her daughter was a nurse, and she wanted to take my blood pressure. Amneh's older daughter really was just studying nursing then, but she had a blood pressure gauge. She took my pressure and said it was high.

That's when Amneh got to work. She brought a handkerchief and tied a knot and put some salt into one corner; then she muttered some prayers and started rubbing the handkerchief around my head. She said it was all because of the Evil Eye, and with Allah's help it would soon be over. She said she was convinced it would work, because she'd yawned as she'd applied the handkerchief, and also because the salt had melted.

The pain persisted, and the hypertension pills didn't help. A month later, on one of my visits home, Father said he thought it had to do with my eyesight. I was having headaches because I was studying so hard, and because all those books and computers must have ruined my eyes. He said a friend of his in Taiyiba, an eye doctor, had told him this. He said the friend's name was Dr. Majed, and he suggested that we go see him at his clinic.

I agreed. The idea of wearing coke-bottle glasses like John Lennon's appealed to me, but I knew how much I really read and how much time I actually spent at the computer.

On our way there, I tried to doze in the backseat. I didn't want Naomi to see me with my eyes swollen again. In fact, Dr. Majed was a psychiatrist, the director of the mental health clinic in Taiyiba. He asked us to come in the afternoon, when there were almost no patients left at the clinic. There was only one woman there, who kept rocking back and forth. Dr. Majed let her in first, renewed her prescription, and then invited us in. With him in the room was a young man, probably an intern, maybe a psychologist. Actually, he may have been a social worker.

Dr. Majed asked me how I was feeling. "Not very well," I answered. He asked if I was having problems at school, and I said everything was great.

Dr. Majed said he had heard from my father that I was in my third year at the boarding school, I was about to start my matriculation exams, I was having recurrent headaches, and the pain was keeping me from concentrating on my studies. Dr. Majed said I was depressed, and prescribed some pills, doxepin 10. "Take one of these a day," he said, "and things will work out fine."

I did, and the pills helped me sleep a little. They made me tired, heavy. My face became bloated, but I felt they were working. I really wanted to be an official depressive like Nick Drake, like Kurt Cobain. I had a renewable prescription, and I got the pills myself. They weren't expensive, and pretty soon I started taking two a day. Then I increased the dose to doxepin 25, and

I got in the habit of popping a pill every time I felt a headache or depression coming on. I walked around in a daze, but nobody asked me why. I'd reached a point where nobody expected any-thing of me anymore, a condition where it's best not to interfere.

Naomi came to see me every now and then. She said she was planning to study psychology. She was going to ask for a deferral of her army service so she could study first, and she had to get good grades on her finals. When the exams were over, we'd split up; I knew that. That's what her mother wanted. She said boarding school was a world apart, and as long as we were there she didn't mind that her daughter had an Arab boyfriend. She said she had nothing against me, except it was too bad my name wasn't Reuben or David.

On the day before the final in Arabic and two days be-fore the last exam in math, I swallowed a whole pack of doxepin 25, ten pills at once. I wanted to sleep. Naomi came to my room. She knocked on the door and I didn't hear her. She knew I was there. I hardly got out of bed in those days. Where would I go anyway? She opened the door and tried to wake me. I could hear her, I could see her, I woke up, but for some reason she thought I was still asleep. I saw her run out and return with the guidance counselor. What was the guidance counselor doing at school at that hour?

Today we had an appointment at the mental health clinic in Jerusalem, with the psychologist in charge of the adolescents' clinic. My parents were told they had to come.

"What are you going to tell them?" my father asks. "Did you tell the guidance counselor anything? Did you talk to them about me?" He mentions Bassem and says he knows about how I've screwed up my studies and ruined everything on account of some girl.

I tell my father I haven't told them anything because there's nothing to tell.

He calms down when he realizes he's not going to come under attack, and nobody is about to blame him for my condition. He'll emerge from the whole thing with his reputation intact. As always.

My mother tries to say everything's going to be okay and I should still consider taking the matriculation exams, but that whatever I decide will be all right, because she's sure I'll manage. She says she doesn't understand how I wound up like this. "We knew you had it tough," she says, "but we didn't realize it was this bad."

I hear them talk. They're interfering with my attempts to concentrate in the backseat, to think about how I have only one more day to see Naomi. To try to imagine our last kiss.

My father launches into another monologue. He says everything he did was for me, to educate me. "Do you know that in England you're allowed to hit schoolchildren to this very day? It's an educational approach."

I tell him I know, I understand, and I swear I haven't said anything to anyone. I've never talked about it.

He believes me again and drops the subject.

And then I remember how on my last visit home on *'id el-adha* he yelled at me. "You lunatic!" he screamed. "You certified lunatic!" All this because I didn't want to pay the usual visit to my aunts. I can still feel my left cheek burning, as if the slap happened just now. I shake my head and put my cheek against the car window to relieve the pain.

I remember the day when Naomi leaned her head against my shoulder for the first time. It was before she told me she loved me, before we started going together. It's hard to reconstruct that feeling. You can remember it, but you can't re-feel it.

Last week, I put my head against her chest, and she ran her fingers through my hair and said, "We shouldn't get too attached, you know. Do you understand? We shouldn't. Enough. We're breaking up, and that's that. Otherwise, Mother will throw me out of the house." She told me her mother had said she'd rather have a lesbian for a daughter than one who hangs out with Arabs.

Suddenly I realize I haven't a clue as to what I'm going to do about the math final, and I'd dropped out of the physics exam too at the last minute. After three years of torture in physics classes, I didn't make it to the exam. Now it hits me: I'm going to flunk. I'm not sure I'll even get my matriculation certificate. My parents will freak out. My father will never get over the shame. He's right, my father. I've ruined my future, and it's all because of the Jewish whore.

But I'm not mad at her, not at all. It's entirely her mother's fault. What could Naomi do about it anyway? If it had been up to her, she wouldn't have broken up with me like that, because how can you stop loving someone overnight, to keep a deadline that was set eighteen months earlier? I had been expecting it the whole time, dreading it.

How I screamed yesterday! What a racket I made! I tried to run away from the emergency room, but the guidance counselor was strong enough to grab me by the arms. When I tried to break loose, I fell to the floor. She kept clutching me by my clothing and whispering, "You're not a child. Stop screaming. Look what you're doing." I remember lots of people just stood around and stared at us, and the guard came but didn't do anything, just stood to the side and watched me cry and scream. When my parents and Bassem arrived, I stopped at once.

The last thing I heard was what my father said to his friend about the Jewish whore. How I hated him then. And I hated the guidance counselor even more. She wanted me to stop loving Naomi, or at least try to love Salwa, an Arab girl at school. She was pretty and smart, that's what the counselor kept telling me. So there I was, on my way back to Jerusalem with my parents. They'd gotten a call from my school, asking them to come with me. I wouldn't be allowed back in school unless my parents and I met with a psychologist first. There wasn't much time left—just one more day and one more matriculation exam—but the counselor said they couldn't assume responsibility for me without the psychologist's approval.

The psychologist said I was okay, I hadn't really wanted to die, and the pills I took wouldn't have hurt me. He believed me when I said I'd read in a book on pharmaceuticals that you need to take as much as 300 milligrams for it to work. He said the information was correct and he was inclined to believe that it wasn't a suicide attempt. He wanted me to have the pills, but he'd give them to the guidance counselor, and she'd give me one a day, because I was still depressed, and it was a psychiatric prescription, after all.

I have to get back to school. There's only one day left.

We didn't talk on the way back to school. We got in the car, same as before. My father fiddled with the dial, looking for the music channel, and swore at Jerusalem for having such lousy reception. He stopped at a steak house for a hummus and a beer. Mother ordered chicken. I didn't want anything. All I wanted was to get back there, so I could see Naomi. I didn't have time to spare. My father looked at me and said, "This is too good for you."

PART FOUR

Hitting Rock Bottom

Chest Pains

I'm walking up the hill that stretches between our house and the mosque, keeping my eyes to the ground, hoping the neighbors passing by have forgotten me by now. Maybe I've changed, and they won't recognize me anymore. I don't exchange the usual *salaam aleikum*s. I shift my side pack from arm to arm. It's heavy, and the trek up toward the taxi station is hard going. Normally Father would drive me there. Sometimes he'd take me as far as Kfar Sava, and the first few times, even to Jerusalem. But Father isn't home now. He's in the hospital.

When Mother got home, I woke up. She explained that Father hadn't felt well the night before, and even though they didn't find anything, they decided to keep him at the hospital for observation. She said there was nothing wrong with him and he'd be discharged soon. If she hadn't needed to get to work by eight, she would have stayed there till they sent him home. She suggested I stop at the hospital to see him on my way to Jerusalem. I had to go through Kfar Sava anyway to catch the bus. "Sit with him for five minutes," she said. She was always trying to mediate between Father and me, to improve our relationship.

Six months had gone by since I'd finished school, six months since my last visit home. Father had tried hard to be nonchalant at first, as if he didn't really care what was happening with me, as if I could go to hell for all he cared. But when he recalled how I'd disgraced him, he'd go berserk and start shouting. "You, our greatest hope, aren't you ashamed of yourself? Everyone in the village keeps asking me how far you've gone. What am I supposed to tell them, that you haven't even taken your finals?" All the other parents are celebrating their kids' acceptance into medical school or law or engineering, and my father has to tell people that the Jews haven't decided yet what to do with my brain. He's told everyone they're afraid another country will kidnap me and use my talents.

I don't have a place of my own in the house anymore. My older brother has put our two beds together to make a queen-size. Whenever I used to come home, Mother would separate the beds and make mine up. But this time she didn't, and they didn't clear any space for me in the closet either. I left my clothes in my side pack and slept in Grandma's room. On a mattress, not in her bed. In the morning, I took my bag and headed for Jerusalem to look for a job. At night, I plan to crash at Adel's. He's in law school already, and he has a room in the dorms.

* * *

Mother called four days ago and said my cousin had been killed. "You've got to come home for the funeral and the three days of mourning." She said he'd been playing ball with a few classmates, and it got on the nerves of their crazy drug-addict neighbors. The ball went over the fence and landed in the druggies' house. The three brothers stormed out with knives and stabbed the kids. Ali was the only one who died. The other kids were injured, but they're okay. My mother said Ali's father was stabbed in the chest when he tried to protect the kids. He was in bad shape, but he'd been operated on, and he'd be all right. They hadn't told him yet. They pretended Ali was okay and had been sent to a different hospital. The doctors said it would be dangerous to give him the news of his son's death at that point. My parents went to visit him in the hospital yesterday. While they were there, at my uncle's bedside, my father complained of chest pains. The doctors decided to do some tests. The tests were okay. Mother says it's just fatigue.

I didn't talk with my father during the days of mourning. He was too busy. Yesterday was the third day. The women sat in my aunt's house, and the men came to ours. The relatives from Ramallah and Bakat el-Hatab slept over and joined us in greeting the people who came to extend their condolences. It was a tragedy. They talked about it on the evening news in Arabic: the cold-blooded murder of a boy playing ball. My job was to stand at the entrance with little cups of coffee and a large coffeepot and pour bitter *sada* coffee for everyone who arrived. My father just sat there the whole time. He cried at Ali's funeral.

Later I heard him say it was the first time he'd ever cried over someone who'd died.

I go up to the fifth floor, into the cardiology ward, and look for room 12. If my father asks, I'll tell him my studies are going well and I'm about to complete my final. I really am studying. If everything continues smoothly, I'll enroll in one of the departments at Hebrew University next year. Not anything exciting, because my grades aren't high enough, but it hardly matters anymore. The main thing is I'll have a degree.

My father is in the bed nearest the door, drinking coffee. He greets me with a surprised *Ahalan,* and I get the feeling he's glad to see me. He asks if I'm on my way back to Jerusalem and says he's got to have a cigarette. Then he asks me to go down to the newsstand to get him a paper, and we'll look for a place where he can read the paper and smoke.

He looks fine, nothing out of the ordinary, hooked up to a flickering machine that's monitoring something, and that's all. I'll get the paper. I'll ask if he needs anything else, and then I'll leave. I'm working today. Besides, I need to get away from this atmosphere. I've got a headache already.

Those three days were rough. It was the first time I'd seen a dead body. I hadn't realized how much Ali had grown. The mustache over his upper lip was beginning to show. The body was naked, with an autopsy incision stretching from his stomach to his neck. Too bad I saw it. The incision had been sewn up hastily with coarse black thread. When the body washers ran out of water, they shoved a bucket in my hand and asked me to hurry. When I realized I couldn't take it anymore, I got out of there and headed home. I said I was going to help set up the chairs and make coffee.

After the funeral, all the men in the family gathered at our house and talked about revenge. The relatives from the West Bank said they would do anything, but there was nobody to kill. The three druggie brothers had been arrested, and the police had moved the rest of their family to a different village. Most of the adults in our family stayed put, while a few of the younger ones huddled in the corner, whispering. My father was older, but he joined them. It was obvious they were planning something. Aunt Fahten walked over to the mourners' tent where the men were seated. She was allowed in there, because she was a widow. She's a strong woman, and wise. She stood in the middle and shouted, "There won't be a single man among you unless you find a way of consoling Ali's mother! Unless you do something that will comfort her!"

The stream of callers didn't let up. From time to time, I switched places with my older brother. He poured the coffee and I washed the dishes. My father was busy the whole time. He never just sat in the tent. He kept going in and out of the house through the back door. He took a few bus trips, car trips too. Around 8 P.M. he came down to the shed, and a few seconds after he sat down we heard a loud boom. Father had a proud look in his eyes. Soon a young guy came in and whispered something to him. Father left the shed again, took the car, and came back within five minutes with two doctors who were relatives of ours. They came with their bags. Someone had been injured out there, but taking him to the hospital was not an option.

I went indoors now too. I didn't know the person who'd been hurt, but I saw he was wearing my father's sneakers. He had a gash in his leg from jumping out the window, but he'd be all right. The callers whispered to one another, trying to figure out what had happened. Soon they realized that the murderers' home had been blown up using the containers of cooking gas.

I come back with the paper. My father's in bed. When he sees me, he sits up and is about to get to his feet. Suddenly he looks at me with big bulging eyes—frightened, imploring eyes. All at once his forehead is covered in perspiration, and the monitor starts beeping nervously.

I scream to one of the nurses, "My father! My father!" and within seconds there's a whole team around his bed. They hook him up to oxygen and pull his bed out toward Intensive Care. I follow them, trying to see his face, but I can't. I can't get into the elevator with them. I run down the stairs and get to Intensive Care before they do. I'm convinced he's dead by now. That's it. There's no hope. He won't make it. I start crying. I head for the phone booths next to the elevators. If he doesn't die now, I'll stay with him right here in the hospital till the next heart attack kills him.

Half the family arrives, my aunts and their children. My mother is wearing a head scarf. Her eyes are swollen from crying. She heads straight for Intensive Care, and there's no stopping her. A few of the men want to talk to a doctor, and they ask for someone to come out and tell them what's happening. They've left their shops, their classrooms, and their businesses to come here. That's all we need now, another tragedy in the family.

The doctor says Father will be okay, but I don't believe it. I saw him perspiring. I saw his eyes telling me he won't be back, he's somewhere else already. They're allowing me in too now. He's still alive, but I know it won't last. They've hooked him up to lots more instruments. The doctor says it wasn't a heart attack, just chest pains. To be on the safe side, they're leaving him in Intensive Care till they run some more tests. I look at him, and he still looks scared, baffled by what he's been through. He looks at me, then at Mother, and I know it's all because of me.

Arabs Called Me a Settler

Arabs called me a settler, their label for anyone who moved into a room that already had two tenants. A third roommate. A squatter. In the Hebrew University dorms, settlers were a big and legitimate group. The rent would be divided three ways, and almost every Arab student welcomed the arrangement. There were just a few city types, mostly from Nazareth, who came to the university in their own cars and didn't want any settlers in their rooms.

The settlers were usually students who'd been late signing up for the dorms or who'd dragged out their studies for too many years and were no longer eligible for a dorm room. There were only two beds in each room, and when both of them were occupied, the settler would bed down on a mattress. I was the only settler who wasn't a student. To get into the dorms, which were closely guarded by security guards—some Jewish, some Druze—you had to produce a student ID. Adel gave me his. He told the administration he'd lost it, and I paid the fine for him and gave him the money for a passport photo.

I found a job within a week. It wasn't hard. In Jerusalem, there are lots of institutions for people with special needs, and they're always short of attendants. The Jews preferred Arabs who had a blue ID card and could get to work even when there were roadblocks, curfews, or war; not like the Arabs from the West Bank with their orange IDs. This was toward the end of the first Intifada, and the orange ones missed many days of work.

I started working at an institution for the retarded. On my shift, I was responsible for six children, some with Down syndrome and others with different conditions. The retarded kids didn't like me, and I didn't like them either. I took them to the bathroom, scrubbed them with a brush, and made sure they were clean. When the girls had their period, I sprayed water on them from a distance. I took them to the dining room, to the occupational workshops, and to the depressing playground. Sometimes, I simply took them on walks through the long buildings. The smell there was terrible, but somehow I got used to it.

I worked every day, and on weekends I'd do a double shift. The pay was very low, and you couldn't really make a decent salary without the overtime and the extra pay on Saturdays. I didn't have much to do anyway. I didn't know anyone except Adel, and I didn't see much of him either, because he was deep in his law studies and I was stuck at work.

Sometimes, when both of us had a free evening, we'd go down to the grocery store, buy some of the cheapest wine with the highest alcohol content, and drink it in the parking lot of the dorms. He always wanted me to tell him what it was like to fuck, and he kept talking about girls. In the end, we'd both

throw up and go back to the room, and if one of the legal occu-
pants was out, we'd share the bed.

Sometimes, when I didn't want to go back to the dorms, I'd go
to the university, look for the psych department, and wait outside for Naomi. I had tried to talk to her at first, to tell her I
had a job, and money, and might invite her to a restaurant sometime. But she was always busy. Sometimes I followed her from
a distance and tried to find out whether she had a new boyfriend yet. I wanted to know if she was as unhappy as I was.
Maybe she still loved me and missed me; maybe it was only
because of her mother that we'd split up. But she almost always
looked happy, and she was surrounded by friends as she went
to the cafeteria or the library.

I had a bus pass from my job, and I would travel around
for hours on the buses, listening to my Walkman and staring
at the people, the shop windows, the cars. I got on and off
whenever I felt like it. I made a point not to keep taking the
same bus, because I didn't want the drivers or the regular passengers to notice me. Sometimes I'd be lost in thought or else
I'd fall asleep, and the driver would wake me with a shout when
we reached the end of the line.

I knew all the bus routes. I knew where each bus went,
and which streets it went through. I studied every way of getting from the dorms to work. I knew the timetables by heart
too, and all the drivers' faces. I started avoiding eye contact when
I got on the bus, because I was beginning to feel as if I knew

them a bit too well. I knew where there would be traffic jams, where the old people would get on, or the children, or the religious people, and which routes were used by Arabs. Sometimes I tried to guess where the passengers were going. To work? To school? To the souk? To the hospital? Sometimes I wanted to know where one of the passengers lived, and I'd get off with him and follow him from a distance with my Walkman on. Sometimes I'd go as far as my school and head right back.

Adel helped me with the math final. It wasn't hard. I took the test and signed up for the two courses with the easiest admission requirements. Sometimes I'd have a cutlet and rice at the university cafeteria. I never thought about the war in those days.

That Morning I Got Up, Made Some Coffee, and Decided to Get Married

I t had been four years since I'd spotted Samia in the bus station near the dorms. She was a refugee but with a blue ID, which meant their village had been destroyed in the war, and some of her family had wound up in Tira. I recognized her and she recognized me. We'd gone to the same elementary school, but had not been in the same class. We'd never talked. I shook her hand and introduced myself, and she smiled. Said she knew me. She looks okay, I thought. I got on the bus before her and took my seat in the back. I was hoping she'd sit down next to me, and she did. I never would have dared to sit down next to an Arab girl. I'm well-behaved and shy.

"Do you know how I get to Hadassah?" she asked.

"Yes, you go to the central bus station and take the Twenty-seven to the end of the line. I'll go with you," I answered.

It was her first day in Jerusalem. I knew she needed me. I was an expert, I knew everything there was to know about public transportation, and the names of streets and places in Jerusalem. I could show her around, maybe do the Old City, even though I didn't enjoy going there, but I'd take her wherever she wanted, even to *El-Aqsa*, if that's what she felt like doing. I'd buy her a present. I'd show her what a good person I was, even if I had screwed up now and then, especially when it came to school.

She'd understand that I've had it rough, that I've been depressed. Maybe she's been depressed too. She only knows me from Tira. She knows I'm smart. She'll be surprised to hear I'm studying philosophy, and I'll tell her it's because I love the subject, and that the job market in hospitals and lawyers' offices is very tight. But she'll probably wind up dating a medical student. That's how it is; doctors marry nurses. I'll tell her I intend to do a doctorate in philosophy.

After we got off, I walked her to the Twenty-seven bus stop, and waited with her till the bus arrived. I knew what it was like to take your first bus trip on a Jerusalem line. Before we said good-bye she told me where she lived, and I gave her my room number. As soon as I got back to the dorms I went looking for her room in the long and narrow buildings. She wasn't there.

How did I even dare? Idiot. What could I have been thinking? In the end, she won't want to see me, and I'll get into trouble. I'll fall in love just the way I did the last time. I won't be able to keep my mind on anything else, and I'll screw up my studies again. I'm going to blow this new chance to prove that I can still make it, that I can take exams the way I used to and get the best grades. I haven't recovered yet from the previous fiasco, and here I am repeating it. I'll never learn.

When I got back to my room, Samia was on the stairs. "I've been looking for you," she said. "It took me an hour to find the room."

✳   ✳   ✳

We've been together for four years now. It's about time. I'll drink my coffee; then I'll wake Samia up and tell her we're going to be married. Until yesterday she was living in the dorms and I was living in the Nahlaot neighborhood with Jewish room-mates. Now that I've moved into an Arab neighborhood, we've got to get married if I want us to go on sleeping together. The owners, who live upstairs, would never allow us to sleep together unless we're married. That's it. We've got to do it. I know she'll never ever leave me, so why put it off?

I didn't know anymore back then whether she was stay-ing with me because she loved me or in order to make it clear to me that I should forget about her ever leaving me. She kept saying I'd promised her we'd get married. I would never break that kind of a promise. It could wreck her life. Everyone in Tira knew by now that we were together, and it was all because of my lack of consideration. As far as she was concerned, she shouldn't be walking hand in hand with me, let alone sleeping with me. She told me that a Tira bride who isn't a virgin is sent back to her parents on her wedding night. Once, her aunt had a heart attack when a daughter of hers showed up at home on her wedding night, but all the bride wanted to do was to pick up her hairbrush.

I couldn't believe Samia'd work up the courage to sleep at my place on that first night in the Arab neighborhood. She cleaned the house, and we told the owner we were engaged. With Jewish owners, we wouldn't have had to explain. Samia used to visit me in Nahlaot and slept over whenever she felt like it. My roommates liked her, and for them it was natural. Not like with the Arabs in the dorms, always gossiping and spreading rumors. Well-founded rumors, but what business was it of theirs? "You, what's it to you? You're a man. What's the worst that could happen to you?" she always said.

Samia has one more term paper to submit. Then she'll go back to Tira, because what would an Arab girl be doing away from her own village? Her father has already found her a job in the municipality. She says there's nothing for her in Jerusalem. And her parents are already suspicious of her latest excuse, the term paper. They say she could be working on it at home.

I look at her in her sleep. Pretty. Facing the wall, as always. It's still early, and she spent all of yesterday cleaning, while I connected the appliances and opened the extra bed I'd bought long ago.

"Get up," I say. "We're going home to get married."

"What, now?"

So I took two days off from work and went home to be married.

My father had no objection to the wedding, quite the contrary. He liked the idea. He didn't mind that I was only twenty-two. He said Samia is from a good family. Communists. Friends of his.

My mother is happy: a girl with a diploma. Maybe she'll reform me too. Maybe she'll gradually succeed in persuading me to go back to the university. "How many courses do you have left? Isn't it a shame for those three years to go down the drain?

Aren't you ashamed of yourself, to have a wife who's better educated than you are? I have to hand it to her for agreeing."

My grandmother knows the refugees. Used to work with them picking fruit. "They're the best women in the village," she says. "Bring her here so I can see her." Even though she can hardly see anymore.

Father says nobody in Tira gets married this way. "It can't be done in two days. Even if we agree, her parents won't. They have their self-respect, don't they?" He says we won't succeed in finding a hall overnight or inviting people. And I explain that I want it to be small. As far as I'm concerned, the only person we need at the wedding is the sheikh. But my parents wouldn't dream of having anyone badmouth them or give anyone a pretext for saying they're not as good as everyone else. "Isn't it bad enough that the poor girl is marrying someone with no home of his own? Are you sure her parents agree?"

Samia's parents agree because they have no choice. The rumors have finished them off already. Her mother had gone to pay a condolence call and overheard people discussing her promiscuous daughter who was studying in Jerusalem. In the mosque where her father prays every Friday, they mentioned her in the sermon. Not by name, but they spoke of parents who send their daughters off to university, where they turn into prostitutes.

My parents won't give up. They settle on one hundred guests on each side, and Father closes a deal with a restaurant owner. They buy gold the way people used to in Tira, and give us money to buy clothes in Tel Aviv. Samia buys a dress on

Shenkin Street, and I get a suit at Zara in Dizengoff Center. Nobody in either one of the families understands why we're getting married like this. The sheikh arrives and I sign his papers seven times. Her father signs for her, which is the custom. We're married now, and all I want is for everyone to finish eating so we can go home.

The next day, my mother called and said the teachers where she worked, the ones who hadn't been invited, thought it was a shotgun wedding and we were just trying to avoid disgrace. Samia said her family hadn't been sure if it was an engagement or a wedding, because at an engagement you only serve *knaffeh* but the restaurant had served a full meal. On the other hand, at a wedding you wear a bridal gown, but she'd worn a dress from Shenkin Street. Samia cried and said it was all my fault. She knew it wouldn't work, I couldn't think of anyone but myself, I wasn't prepared to do anything for her, and her parents were hurt and angry because she hadn't been married like everyone else.

My father chewed me out too. He said I was a mess. "Next week come again, and we'll put an end to this disgrace."

So we got married all over again. The checks covered the hall, the music, the photographer, a thousand guests, and a Netanya hotel. Apart from my aunts and their children, I hardly even knew anyone at my own wedding. I hadn't invited anyone.

Everyone had been invited by my parents or Samia's. I put on my black suit and my black shoes, like in an Arab movie. I had to put the ring on Samia's finger. I had to dance with her, even though I haven't a clue about dancing the *debka*. I was supposed to cut the cake and kiss men whose names I didn't know. I had to hug my aunts and uncles and smile at the camera. I had to listen to horrible music that never fails to give me a headache. And I had to put up with all that without any alcohol or ciga- rettes. Because I'm well-behaved and shy.

Beit Safafa

few months after we got married for the second time, we moved into Beit Safafa. It used to be a village, but by then it was a neighborhood of Jerusalem. It's good to be a stranger. Nobody follows you around. Nobody takes an interest in you, and the only thing the landlord cares about is that you pay the rent on time. True, our landlords are Arabs, but we still don't feel like we belong. We have no relatives or acquaintances or friends here the way we do in Tira.

Our house is in an area that was occupied in 1967. Its Hebrew name is Givat Ha-Matos (Hill of the Plane), because an Israeli plane was downed there in the war. From 1948 to 1967 there'd been a barbed wire fence running through the village, splitting it in two. For nineteen years, brothers, relatives, and families living on either side of the fence couldn't visit each other. Our landlady says that the only time the Israelis and the Jordanians would allow families to approach the fence and shake hands with two fingers was on holidays or wedding days. She showed us pictures of a wedding being celebrated on both sides of the fence. Half the family lived in Jordan and the other half in Israel, she said, and laughed. Now both halves are occupied by Israel, except that people in the part occupied in '67 have residents' passes and those in the part occupied in '48 have citizens' passes, so they're considered superior and more loyal. At least their homes are higher. It figures—they've always had more work on the Israeli side.

My wife and I are citizens, and thanks to that our land-lady treats us with respect, because we have medical insurance and social security and we know Hebrew well. The homes in the half of the village that was occupied in '67 are cheaper, because there's no sewage system, and the water and electricity are supplied by Arab companies, so there are a lot more power stoppages and problems with the water system. When war broke out—the Intifada—the Palestinian part came under much greater pressure because the electricity was cut every time Israel shelled Bethlehem or Beit Jala or Beit Sahur. There *was* a big settlement separating us from places that were shelled, but we still belonged with the Palestinians, at least when it came to water and electricity. Life became much more difficult with the Intifada, and my wife and I began to regret that we hadn't rented in the Israeli half. The rent's a little higher, but we would have managed with a smaller home.

Since the war broke out, there have been more soldiers milling around in the Palestinian half, and the power cuts are making the winters tougher, especially for the baby. We can hear the shellings, but they haven't reached us so far. The Pal-estinian side of Beit Safafa is quiet, because they know that if they join the Intifada the Arab tenants will move out of the rented apartments, which are their main source of livelihood.

Almost all of the people in the Palestinian half have set aside a room for rental or built an extra home for citizens like us who are trying to leave their own village in favor of the big city. People feel solidarity with the ones who are being shelled just a short distance away, and they take up collections of toys and money for the refugee camps, but they won't throw so much as a single stone at the Jewish soldiers who are underfoot everywhere. It's embarrassing what people will do to make ends meet.

We have a small home. Our daughter sleeps with us in our room, and there's a small kitchen and a small bathroom. When a Jew is killed, our landlady bakes *basbussa* and brings us a portion in a small dish. She takes off her head scarf and stuffs it in her mouth to muffle the sound. Then she gives muted cries of joy.

Our landlady is a refugee from the village of Malcha. Sometimes she climbs up on the roof and looks down at her home. It's still there, two meters away from the mosque. In 1948 she escaped to the southern part of Beit Safafa, which had become Jordanian, and since 1967 she's been working at the Hebrew University. She's head of a department, which means she's in charge of the toilets on the law school campus. When the war broke out, her brother was praying at the El Aqsa Mosque, as he did every Friday—and was killed. He was a plumber, and he had a small Fiat. His sister used to call him every time our pipes were clogged. When our daughter was born, he arrived with his wife and children and brought us a present.

The Fashion Channel

I'm lying on the sofa, trying to entice myself with the fashion channel. Bridal gowns flash in front of me. I try to think back on my own wedding, but I'm too drunk for that. One of the landlord's brothers has just gotten married. They kept the guest list small, with no music and no food. The two families only spent half an hour together.

There's shooting again, and another power cut. It wakes up my wife. I can't understand why it's the quiet that causes her to wake up. Or the darkness. She calls me from the bedroom, trying to talk loud enough for me to hear, but not so loud as to wake the baby. "The flashlight is on the TV," she says.

In summer the shooting and the shelling are louder, especially at night. You sit there trying to imagine exactly where they've landed or to picture the helicopters homing in on a target, tilting downward and shooting. The pilots are the best. They must be my age, but with a good physique and a nice face. They'll finish their nightly assignment, step out of the plane, and take off their helmets, and with an impressive flick of their wrist they'll fix their hair. Fair hair, blond maybe, but it's hard to tell in the dark. Especially since the alcohol throws me off.

Another salvo of shooting. My wife bends over, and her silhouette on the wall frightens me for a moment. "It's as if we don't belong." She yawns. "We're onlookers, like strangers, doing nothing."

"Tomorrow. Tomorrow I'll call the power company," I tell her. "It can't go on this way. I'll sue them."

I'll sue my father too, for planting hope in my mind, for lying to me. For teaching me to sing:

"We'll march through the streets, for united we stand
Let us sing to our glorious nation, our land."

I'll sue him for telling me that the Lebanon War was the great darkness before the great light. I laugh at him when he says, every time they shell Gaza or Ramallah, "That's it, that'll be the end of them." I remember how we once sang to being free and united. Father's voice would rise as we sang:

"Let the revolution come. Let victory be ours."

I can never forgive him for giving us the idea that we'd defeat the enemy with tires and stones.

I haven't an ounce of hope in my heart. I'm filled with hate. I hate my father. Because of him I can't leave this country, because he taught us there was no other place for us, and we must never give up; it would be better to die for the land. I picture him and tell him everything that's on my mind. I say that if it weren't for all the nonsense he drummed into us I would have left long ago. Now he's drunk, like me, but he clings to hope. If he loses that, he'll die. Hope is dwindling, but somewhere it can still be felt. Even when he cries, as Nazareth comes under attack, it sounds like the distress of someone who expects the great redemption to come soon—just the way he described it in what he wrote while he was in detention.

I don't remember the date of the last demonstration I attended. I don't remember what it was about: Land Day, Nakba Day, or just some Arabs who were murdered at some intersection. I remember how my father and his friends worked all night. They drew slogans on big signs. I stood there, bringing them colored markers whenever my father asked me to. The only person I recognized was my math teacher, and he acted as if he didn't know me. They wrote: YA PERES, YA SHARON. THIS IS OUR COUNTRY AND HERE WE ARE. They wrote: THE CHICKEN OF THE GOLAN HEIGHTS IS BEHAVING LIKE A LION IN LEBANON. (Father said it was directed at Assad.) They wrote: REJOICE, O MOTHER OF THE *SHAHID*. ALL CHILDREN ARE YOUR CHILDREN. My father and his friends drew flags of Palestine and asked me and my brothers to color in the squares: green, black, red, and white. That was when I finally learned how to draw a flag, and we fought over which one should be on top, the green or the black. Father said it didn't matter, because it's the thought that counts.

The next day, I couldn't remember what the reason was, but my father said we should be taking part in the demonstration too. A pickup truck with loudspeakers set out from our house, and my brother and I and some of Father's friends followed it with our signs. I could hear his voice over the loudspeakers, and people started joining the group that was marching behind the pickup. It seemed to me that everyone had turned out. The crowd swelled till it turned into an enormous body marching forward. My brothers and I tried to keep our place near the pickup, near Father. When we passed our home again, Mother and Grandma were waiting there with pitchers and bottles of water and gave some to the marchers. Mother said, "May God bless them," and I could tell she was crying. She signaled the pickup to stop and gave my father a drink of cold water from a glass, just the way he liked it.

"What's going to happen?" my wife wants to know. "War?" I wish she'd come back to bed because I've just begun undressing the first female combat pilot.

From the neighborhood up the hill above us we can hear the noise of Jews. Under the streetlights along their road I can see them advancing toward our house. The crowd is growing larger. They're marching down the road above us. The house we've rented is pretty isolated. It's the closest to the Jews. The landlord, who lives above us, knocks on the door and says, with a flashlight in his hand and tension in his face, "The Jews are attacking."

The Jewish voices grow louder. Under the streetlights along their streets I can see them streaming toward our house. It's becoming dangerous, so the landlord invites us to stay in his parents' old home in the center of the village. We'll be better protected there.

My wife starts crying, and I say, "We're going home." I take the baby out of her crib. She screams. I wrap her in her blanket, and we're off. I hope they haven't blocked the exit yet, but if the police cars are there already, I'll tell them I'm a citizen and that I'm only renting here. I'll show them my ID. I got it at the Ministry of Interior in Netanya. I'm not really Palestinian. I'll tell them the baby's sick.

I heave a sigh of relief as we reach the lit-up part of the city. They're not going to recognize me. I'm counting on the fact that I look like a Jew. Let's just hope they don't see my wife. Couldn't I have picked someone with a lighter complexion? She speaks softly to the baby, trying to calm her, and I shout at her to shut her trap if she wants to come out of this alive. The Jews haven't reached the entrance yet, and the ones we meet peer into the car suspiciously, but when they see me they let us go. We've got to get out of here right away. Lucky I'm not one of those who hang prayer beads on the mirror. Lucky I don't have a *hamsa* or letters in Arabic. I've got a pretty Jewish car, a Subaru, not the typical Peugeot or Opel Ascona. I've always known how to make myself inconspicuous.

I turn the dial, skipping over the Arab stations, and select the IDF channel. Then I turn up the volume till we're out of the city. They're burning down mosques. They're shooting at villages and cities. People have been killed. There's a strange pain in my joints. My arms and legs feel hollow, full of cold air, paralyzed.

I drive down the road out of Jerusalem much faster than usual. I've never gone at such speed with my daughter in the car. I'm afraid of crashing on the slopes. The roads don't look any different. Every now and then, there's the light of a passing vehicle and my eyes seek out the trucks carrying the tanks covered in heavy netting and green tarpaulin. I usually speed up once I reach the bottom of the hill, but I'm careful this time, because even the traffic police could be dangerous. That's all I need now, for some cop to ask for my papers and find out who and what I am.

On Days When There Are Terrorist Attacks

On days when there are terrorist attacks, my wife says we've got to start saving. We should stop paying for cable. We could use the money to buy something new each year. Instead of watching TV we could be buying new sofas. She says what we have can hardly pass for a sofa. Besides, we need a new stove. We need a microwave oven to heat up the baby's food. She doesn't want expensive furniture. Even the least expensive will do. She's seen some nice sofas at Golan Furniture in the Talpiyot neighborhood. In any case, since we move every year or two, there's no point buying anything expensive, because the movers ruin the furniture. Last time, they broke the handle off our fridge and never managed to reassemble the cupboard.

My wife says we shouldn't buy good things until we move into our own home in Tira. All we have there for the time being is the shell of a building, but with my parents' help we can finish it within a year. Her father will buy the appliances. That's how it is. The husband builds the home, and the wife buys the appliances. He bought very expensive ones for her younger sister. He's stingy, but he feels compelled to make a good impression on strangers, like I do.

Unless I return to Tira now, my younger brother will get all my parents' savings. He's finished school and he's coming back to the village. He'll join my older brother, who got married six months ago and lives in a house of his own already, behind the one my parents live in: a spacious nice-looking house with a garden. There are two identical shells alongside it—one for me and one for my younger brother. My wife can't understand what I like about being in Beit Safafa, when we're surrounded by the scariest Jews—from Gilo, and the Patt neighborhood, and the Katamon projects. At least in Tira you don't hear shooting or helicopters overhead, and they don't disconnect the electricity every time they shell Beit Jala. She figures she'll work in the municipality. Because she's fed up. Every time there's a terrorist attack, nobody at work will talk to her. She knows they need social workers in Tira. There are plenty of problems and not enough staff.

Before my younger brother got engaged, he asked if I was planning to move back home, because if not, he'd prefer to take over the shell they built for me. It could save him a lot. He wanted to get married quickly. He was engaged to a girl from Karra who went to university with him, and he was finding the distance oppressive. I told him that as far as I was concerned he could have them both, because I was never coming back.

I can't figure out where my father got the money to build three shells. I didn't think he had any money. He'd always complained about the cost of my tuition. He said if I'd been studying something useful he wouldn't have minded so much, but I was just wasting my time. I started working right from my freshman year. I didn't want to live in the dorms, and my father said if I wanted to rent an apartment I'd have to get a job.

We have to save the way your parents did, my wife says. Where do you think they got the money? Sometimes she calculates the value of the property that my parents own—the homes and the land—and says it's worth more than a million dollars. She says I should stop being so naïve. Since my brother's wedding, less than a year ago, they must have saved fifty thousand already. Unless I make a move, I'll be left with nothing. My parents will never just come out and offer me some of it.

When a helicopter hovers over our home, I feel my wife has a point. Maybe it really is time to go back to Tira, to forget about Jerusalem and turn over a new leaf. If I don't go back now, I'll have to wait till they marry off my brother in a fully furnished home. This is my chance. My life there could be better, more focused. My wife says I don't have anything to hide from anymore and nothing to conceal. My drinking and smoking is something my parents know about anyway. And besides, she never could understand why a married man of over twenty-five is afraid his parents will find out he smokes. It wasn't until the day my wife gave birth that I asked my father to lend me a cigarette.

The alcohol I can hide in the cupboard, according to my wife, like my father. He drinks a lot, and there's always a bottle of whiskey waiting in the bedroom. I don't dare help myself, even though I'm often tempted. Once, when Grandma still had the strength, she would look for his bottles and flasks and break them outside. She'd rock the whole neighborhood with her screaming about my father and his irresponsible behavior. Wasting his money on alcohol instead of saving for his children. Who would send them to the university? Who would build them homes? She'd scream till she was red in the face, her voice almost choking. It's all my mother's fault, Grandma would say. She doesn't know how to domesticate her husband. She sits around with him, glad that he drinks. She doesn't care about the children. She spends everything on clothing and restaurants. Instead of every bottle he drinks, instead of every blouse she buys, they could be buying another chicken for the children.

An Arab Lover

Every time I enter the kitchen, I remind myself I need a lover. Even my wife knows. Since she gave birth, she says she doesn't care anymore. As far as she's concerned I can bring one home with me. She says Islam permits such things, something called a *marriage of enjoyment.*

For a few months now, my wife has been saying I can't stand her. That's for sure, I say. I never could stand her, but lately it's worse than ever. She asks what's changed, and I say nothing has changed with me; she's the one who's more sensitive, now that she's a mother.

I'm looking for an Arab lover, preferably a married one, someone who'll understand me. Someone I'll have a lot in common with. She can be a divorcée or an unmarried woman who's been through a lot. I'll put an ad in the paper. How much could it cost? But I'm afraid of ugly ones or of the Arab men who may try to find out who the pervert is. She might send me a letter and a picture to my postal box, or make a date at some café, and just then one of my neighbors will happen to come in and everyone in Beit Safafa will be talking about me.

I'm a failure anyway. One night a cabdriver who took me home asked me my name, and as soon as I told him, he said, "Oh, so you're the one who comes home drunk every night." Lots of taxi drivers from the village work downtown at night. I can see them staring at me as I walk out of the bar, so I start taking out the garbage when I leave, even though I don't have to. That way maybe the cabbies will think I'm working and not just wasting money.

Unfortunately, I've had to rule out the possibility of finding a lover in Beit Safafa itself. Sometimes when we visit Tira, my mother-in-law talks about another married woman who was caught with one of the neighbors or with a stranger. It never fails to surprise me—Arab women who cheat on their husbands. I admire them. The ending is always tragic. They always wind up being caught in one of the orchards of Tel Mond or Ramat Ha Kovesh. The orchards, *el-bayarat,* have always been the scene of forbidden things. I grew up on stories of people being hunted down in orchards or orange groves, of thugs setting fire there to stolen cars, of criminals being found dead or young girls found hanging from the branch of an orange or avocado tree. If it happens in Tira, it probably happens in Beit Safafa too. Except that we're not tuned into the local scene. We're strangers here; we don't know the main characters in the play. There are no orchards or groves, and I've yet to locate the hub of the Arab criminal scene. Sometimes I think it may be at the Malcha shopping mall or at the Biblical Zoo.

When I get myself a lover, I won't know where to take her. All the places I've thought of seem too dangerous, too visible. There are Arabs in all the cafés and all the bars, and working in just about every restaurant in town. Maybe someone will recognize her? Maybe someone has seen me sometime in the past? If I can work up the courage, I'll take my lover to the Jerusalem forest. We'll find a quiet spot or park the car and walk down to one of the side paths. We'll sit there, talking and looking at the view. When it gets dark, we can make out in the car. Just once, I've got to make out in a car. Maybe she'll bring her husband's BMW. Maybe he has a Volvo. But me, I'd never risk going into the forest. What if they stole my car? It'd take us five hours to walk back to town. And what if we're killed by some Arab? Nobody will feel bad about the mistake, not even the Arabs. They'll say it's an omen. God wanted to expose the criminals and punish them. Better die by hanging in the groves of Tel Mond than get shot as a Jew by mistake—and with a lover, no less. How would they be able to tell we were Arabs, sitting in the forest and making out? I'm pretty sure she wouldn't be wearing a veil.

It's not that I'm good-looking. My wife says I'm okay. She says I have no neck and my head is too big. She says I've got to stand up straight when I walk, because it could add five centimeters to my height. At the pharmacy she bought me a device that's supposed to support your back, but it bent out of shape within a week. I'm not fat, but my cheeks are too big. I look in the mirror and see the bulges I should get rid of. They really are ugly, and no matter how much weight I lose they won't go away. My wife says it has to do with the shape of my skull, and nothing is going to change it. I try not to eat too much, and if

I do, I try to throw up as much as possible. I never leave the house, even just to the grocery store, without throwing up first. My wife says my proportions are all wrong. My body's thin and my head's enormous. I've got to gain some weight.

I need a lover quick. How much longer can I last with the same woman? I'm not to blame. They keep talking on TV about the chemical substance of love that stops working after four years with the same person. So according to science, I've been walking around for two and a half years without the chemical substance. Sometimes I think that's why I throw up.

My wife says that unless I change I'll never find a lover. I'm too lazy. I don't even take the trouble to empty an ashtray. I'm too immersed in myself to be able to invest in a lover. "You've got to invest," she says, but I don't know what that means. And she explains, "It means to invest emotionally, but you're not capable of that. As far as you're concerned, anything goes. *Ahalan wa-sahalan.* I wish you had a lover. She'd suffer like hell. At least there'd be one more person who knew what you're like. Maybe she would help me with the baby and the house."

Sometimes my wife says I have a good heart. I'm the kindest person in the world, she says. And sometimes she says I'm as mean as they come, so mean I have no idea what love is all about, and the best thing I could do would be to stay drunk. Now she remembers how I seemed to her back at the beginning. How she liked me then. How I used to go to the supermarket on Fridays to buy tomatoes, lettuce, and cucumbers, to make salad and fry cutlets for her. Now she laughs at herself, for ever believing I really was different.

Not Made for Love

My father always says I have no love in my heart, that I'm not made for love. My wife agrees with him. She's never met anyone as indifferent and inconsiderate as I am. She says I don't even see the other person. As far as I'm concerned, I'm in the center, and the whole universe revolves around me. She says she hates me, that I have no idea how much she hates me. She'd love for them to find I had cancer, so I'd die as soon as possible. She can't stand the sight of me anymore. I'm the most repulsive thing in her life. She wishes I'd die—amen! She won't wait long after I die. She'll remarry quickly. I was the one who made her forget the joy of living. I destroyed her, I shattered her, I turned her into a depressive old lady in her twenties. If only I'd have a traffic accident and get killed. She doesn't want me to wind up disabled. She wants it to be final, wants me to die on the spot. Actually she wouldn't mind if it took me two days to die. Quite the contrary, she'd be pleased if I suffered. Or I could be unconscious, and she'd stand at my hospital bedside, cry, and hold my hand as all the people came to see me for the last time, but when we were alone she'd be happy. She'd be sure I knew how happy she was. She would give a voiceless chuckle and whisper in my ear, "It's what you deserve, you sonofabitch."

How Samia cried when we slept together the first time. The sheet in the dorm room was covered in blood, and she didn't stop crying the rest of the night. She sat on the bed, her knees pulled up, leaning her head on them between her arms, and cried. I was sure she'd cry herself to death. I could tell that something horrifying was about to happen, and there was nothing I could do. I just sat there facing her, helpless, frightened, and kept promising I'd marry her if she wanted. I was prepared to marry her then and there. So what if I was nineteen years old?

She can't leave now. After losing her virginity. They'll kill her, they'll kill me. Nobody will ever marry her. If it isn't me, there'll never be anyone else. Women without their hymen intact are kicked out. What a disgrace. Damaged goods, they have to be discarded. I wouldn't do that to anyone. I'd never let her suffer on my account. I was the one who did it to her, and I'll take responsibility.

"It was a black day," my wife says. "God, what an idiot I was. Damn the circumstances that made me stick it out with you. You animal. Did I say animal? Even an animal has more feelings than you do. I hope you die. I hope I finally get rid of you. There's no point making an effort to love you anymore." And again she curses her parents and her family. They're the reason she can't just dump me. If she had the strength, she'd kill me. She'd grab me by the neck and never let go. She lashes out and slaps the air by way of showing me what she means.

She'd like to bang my head against the wall again and again till it broke. She says I have no idea how much she hates me. Even just looking at me makes her sick. "I hate you, I hate you! You dog. You animal."

Sometimes I think I ought to just throw my clothes in the car and take a few books I read long ago, books I know I used to love, though I can't remember why. I'd fix the car radio and drive off. For a few days in Eilat maybe. I've never been to Eilat. If I had the courage to cross the border, I'd go to the Sinai. And if it weren't for the baby, I'd never come back.

When I grew older, I realized I'd been duped. An Arab girl's hymen wasn't as holy and pure as people said it was. Samia had been doing a number on me. She'd been taking advantage of my naïveté. She'd been exploiting the fact that I didn't know much and filling my head with honor-or-death ideas. Those were years of being afraid, of hiding out. Sometimes I went through an entire night in Nahlaot without sleeping a wink, even though nobody in that neighborhood knew me anyhow. I was sure they'd find me, and once they did it would be the end of me. I never left the door unlocked and never slept with the window open. Not that it would have saved me. If anyone had wanted to get to me, nothing would have stopped them. But I had to try to stop anyone who was likely to arrive on the scene. I had to be there to shout it out: "I'm willing to marry her right away!"

I would never tell my wife "I hope you die," even though I've pictured her dead often enough. I know I wouldn't be able to handle the loss; suddenly, when she disappeared, I'd start loving her, missing her, and understanding how right she was. What a sonofabitch I was. If anything happened to her, I'd blame myself, nobody else. Because I'd wished for it to happen. And I believe wishes do come true in the end.

If Samia dies, I'll visit her grave as often as I can. Not only on holidays, like the other people in the village. At the beginning, I'll go there at least once a week. I'll weep, I'll speak to her, I'll ask her to forgive me, I'll speak words of love. I'll mourn her with all my heart. I'll suffer. I can picture myself sitting there, all by myself in the cemetery on rainy days, in the cold, cocooned in the long black overcoat I don't own. I won't be afraid of going there at night. I'll have a beard, and it will give me an air of suffering, a special aura. I'll cry out at the grave, and people will hear my pain. And every now and then I'll give out a long moan that will echo through every home in Tira.

Hitting Rock Bottom

I think I've hit rock bottom. I've broken almost every rule I can think of in the moral code. I'm going home now, to sleep it off. I'd like the radio to be on in the background as I doze off but I don't have a radio. It broke long ago, and I can't face the idea of having to take it to be fixed or of having to fork out the money for a new one. I'd like to go to sleep now and not have any bad thoughts.

Sometimes I think I know what mental relaxation means. I can outline it in my brain. I know where I'm heading. I'd like to be able to crawl into bed with a book, any book. A book of jokes, maybe, or light stories about Jucha. I'd like to settle into it, to enjoy it, to doze off with a smile on my lips. I'd like the book to slip out of my hands ever so slowly, to fall off the bed without my noticing. I'd like to be tucked in tight with my body at just the right temperature, not too cold and not too hot. I'd like to fall asleep in just the right position. I'd like the pillows to be propped at just the right height. My neck won't hurt and I won't have to move. I won't have any noise in my ears, and my head won't ache either. I'd like to find sublime serenity.

I'd like my wife to be there with me too, to blend with me as we relax and fall asleep. Our bodies will be in sync. She can place her head on my chest. She won't have to twist her neck, and her hair won't get in my eyes or in my mouth. I'll hug her. I'll place a hand under her head, and my arm won't hurt or fall asleep. I'll place one leg on her waist, and it won't be too heavy. It will even make her feel good, give her a warm sensation, round off her own body. Her waist will be a comfortable resting place. It'll be thin and youthful. She'll smile at me and say a heartfelt "I love you" and kiss me. I'll feel the kiss draw me into a delightful childhood dream. I'll smile in my sleep, and my wife will smile back and fall asleep.

The baby will sleep, knowing she has loving parents that she can always count on. She'll have an angelic smile and a dry diaper. She'll be eager to talk, to tell us how wonderful we are, how much she loves us. She won't have a rash or an eye infection, and she'll never ever cry. She won't be bored. She'll feel wonderful; she'll be happy to be alive. She'll sleep till morning and wake us at just the right moment with little giggles and her first word. *Baba,* maybe. My wife will be happy for me. She'll hug me and tell me she's always known that the baby would say my name first, because I'm so good to her. I shower her with love.

I'll give up drinking. Just a glass of wine on Friday night. I'll buy a good bottle of wine in a liquor store, not a supermarket. A store in a good neighborhood. Not the kind that sells mostly to Romanian workers, not one that sells Gold Star Beer. We'll have a set of wineglasses that we'll receive from our parents. A bottle is too much for two so we'll invite a couple we know. We'll enjoy a good meal together. We'll be comfortably full, with no stomachaches. Nobody will need to use the bathroom. We'll eat just the right amount and we won't grow a potbelly. The wine will go well with the meal. Maybe a piece of fine cake too, to enhance the pleasurable experience. It'll melt in our mouths. It won't stick to our teeth, and it'll be digested smoothly, with no pangs of conscience.

I won't have any more thoughts about women. I won't keep looking at every girl's ass. I'll treat women with respect and listen to them without thinking dirty thoughts. I'll stop jerking off. I won't keep looking for tits and fucks on TV, and if there happen to be any in the middle of a good film, I'll treat them like art. It won't turn me on. My hands will always be where they belong. It'll be good with my wife. She'll know exactly what I want. I like her, I love her, I lust for nobody but her: her long neck, her Gypsy face, her perfect figure. We'll understand each other. We'll take each other's needs into consideration. We'll always come at the right moment, and we'll want to do it again. There will be nights when we won't get to sleep at all. We'll make love until sunrise. She won't dry out, and I won't let her down.

I'll go home now. I'll drive slowly, in the right gear. I won't overload the engine. I've got to be as quiet as possible. I hope none of our neighbors is making his way to morning prayers just now. I hope it's still early enough, I hope there are no workers waiting at the intersection. I'll keep my eyes to the ground. I won't smoke a cigarette, I won't listen to music. I'll go to sleep now, and tomorrow will be a new day. I'll show them all.

Tomorrow I'll start praying. I've forgotten how you wash before prayers and what you say. I don't remember the right sequence, or the number of prayers you're supposed to say. Tomorrow I'll buy an instruction book with pictures, the kind we had in elementary school. I'm convinced I wouldn't be in this condition if only I'd kept on praying. Look at me, look at what's become of me. Me, the one everyone expected to succeed. What a comedown. I'm going to prove to myself that I'm a good person, and then I'm going home to Tira.

I have no idea what I'm going to do there. It's certainly not a place for a barman. They don't even have alcohol. My father says I ought to become a social worker. They don't have enough social workers in Tira. I could go to the same place as my wife every morning, and come back home with her in the evening. Maybe I'll become a teacher. If I start praying tomorrow, I may still stand a chance of becoming a teacher of religion. Maybe I'll be accepted into the A-Shari'a College in Hebron. It's easy to get in, and they need lots of teachers of religion. I'll be a good teacher. I've been through a lot in my life, and I can help keep my students on the straight and narrow. I'll make sure they don't go downhill the way I did. I'll warn them against what can happen, but I won't tell them how far gone I was. I'll have the reputation of a good person. People will come to consult with me on questions of religious law. They'll listen to what

I tell them, they'll respect me, and they'll follow my advice. My father will be proud. He'll start praying too. Perhaps we'll go on a pilgrimage to Mecca together.

Gradually I'll blend into the local political scene, and when my students get the right to vote they'll nominate me for the Islamic ticket. They'll make sure I'm at the head of the party list, and in the following elections I'll be elected mayor.

I'll be a candidate selected by consensus. I'll be a Member of Knesset. The media will love me. They'll find it hard to believe that a Moslem MK can talk like that, without a trace of fanaticism, gently, almost without an accent. I'll express myself well, and I'll represent the views of an entire community. Even the Jews will consider me an honest man. I'll get along very well with the right-wing parties and the ultra-orthodox. I'll become prime minister—the first Arab in the Islamic Movement to be made prime minister. I'll bring peace and love to the region. The economy will flourish. There will be no war on the horizon. I'll turn the Middle East into a superpower. I'll be head of the Asian Union, and Israel will market *maklubah, za'atar,* and gefilte fish in New York's fanciest malls. The naked girl I left behind yesterday will never believe it. She slept with the mightiest leader in the world!

The Night of Purim

I t's the night of Purim, and two Arabs are taking over the dance floor. "They shouldn't let Arabs dance here," I tell Shadia, who's standing there with me behind the bar. She chuckles and agrees with me. "It's disgusting. In Nejaidat or any other village like that, people like that would be raped. I'm telling you, they simply grab those kinds of people and fuck them whenever they want to."

They really are ugly, especially the short one with the mustache. He swivels his ass, crammed into those cloth pants of his, making a mockery not only of himself but of anyone dancing next to him—of the whole bar, especially Shadia and me. If he wasn't so clueless, he wouldn't dare to dance. Why should Arabs like him be dancing disco anyway? Don't they realize how different they are, how out of place, how ugly? Especially the short one with the mustache. He doesn't give up. Just keeps popping peanuts into his mouth and shaking his ass. Thinks he's a regular celebrity model, and every girl dancing near him is a whore. Every time the ugly dwarf orders another beer, he points at one of the girls and says, "She's Russian, isn't she?"

"It's my last shift," Shadia says. "I can't stand the sight of this place anymore. I can't stand the sight of all these Arabs. They've destroyed the place, they've driven out the paying customers. The ugliest people in Jerusalem come here, good-for-nothings who think they're God. I swear I feel like calling in a few people from Nejaidat, just to come in here and knock these guys senseless, the little shits. Especially the one with the mustache." She giggles and covers her mouth with the back of her hand.

Shadia was the first Arab girl I'd met who knew about Tom Waits. She happened to sit next to me at one of the lectures in the philosophy department seven years ago. I was putting a new cassette in my Walkman, and she recognized it. That changed my whole perception of Arabs. Because of her, I realized there's a different kind; they're not all the same. But apart from her, I've yet to meet an Arab who likes the same music I do.

She lives in the Old City and only goes back to Nejaidat on holidays. She says nobody in her family will talk to her. Every time she goes there she imagines it'll be different, and then she sinks back into her depression. She wrote a book and sent it to several publishers in Egypt but never got an answer. She doesn't think they'll accept it; her writing is too difficult for them to digest. Only two people liked what she wrote. One of them is dead already, and the other was Mahmoud Darwish. She says she'd always wanted to write about her childhood, but the problem was that sometimes in Nejaidat a whole week would go by with nothing happening. People would pass one another from time to time and ask, "How're things?" and they'd answer, *El-hamdulila.*

"How many times can I write *el-hamdulila* in the same book?" She smiles. "I spent the whole year writing, for hours on end, day in and day out. But when all was said and done, my entire childhood took up barely forty pages."

She'll quit her job at the bar. Maybe she'll go to New Zealand. She gets along well with sheep. She doesn't stand a chance here. She can't find a job. She worked for a while as curator at a prestigious Ramallah gallery, but there's a war on now. Everyone at the bar comes on to her, especially the Arabs. They think they're really sophisticated when they say, "Give me an orgasm."

She can't stand it anymore, the way they look at her. As if because she's an Arab and she works at a bar, she must be a whore. If anyone says anything, she gives him a really hard time. She raises the roof with her screaming. The last thing she needs is for false rumors to reach the people back in Nejaidat. Even in the streets of the Old City, if anyone says anything as she passes by, she walks back and knocks him over with her yelling.

Shadia carries a knife around with her; she stole it when she was in first grade. When there are problems, she hides the knife up her sleeve. It's a switchblade, not like my Lederman with its nail clipper, its screwdrivers, and its spoon. Shadia laughs at me when I tell her about my knife. She says she could write a good story about these things—about an Ashkenazi nerd who entered the world of crime. There was a guy called Husni in her class. He'd robbed a bank once. She couldn't believe he did it. He wasn't capable of stealing an eraser. Someone shot him when he came out with the money, just some sonofabitch with a pistol. A Jew. They didn't do anything to him, didn't even arrest him.

It was her last shift. She couldn't go on this way anymore. It was the night of Purim and the place was so sad. Not a single good-looking person. The regulars come in, take a look around, and leave. I can understand them. I'd never go to a place where the dancers were so ugly. Shadia and I don't dance like them and we don't look like them, and both of us arrived with a premonition. It was Purim night and we smelled trouble. For the first time, I was wandering around with something in my pocket that could open into a knife.

"The owner had better pay a bouncer to get them out of here," she says, and I nod. "I for one would never come back here. And I don't mind having to pay for my own liquor. What about you? Are you staying?"

I look at the bar, at the beer stains, the lemon, the lupine spikes in the ashtrays. We're not emptying the ashtrays today. We don't want anyone to stay. Facing me at the bar is a man in a suit. He must be past fifty. Sometimes he says he's a lawyer, sometimes he tells us he studied medicine in Frankfurt. He orders another glass of white wine, and as he puts it to his thick lips, it brings out the deep wrinkles in his rugged complexion. Like cracks in the desert soil after an earthquake. Now he's putting on his glasses to write down a phone number for the girl next to him. She's a stranger, a volunteer in one of the human rights organizations. She's short and heavy-set, looking for men the whole time and not particular.

There's no way I can look like them. If I convey what these Arabs convey, I'm in serious trouble. But it's out of the question. People aren't scared of me, and they're not put off by me. Or maybe they are, except they manage to hide it. I bet there are lots of girls who got the wrong idea, as if I was coming on to them, and I must have been as disgusting as the rest of them. I can't believe it.

Every time our paths cross, Shadia and I manage to pick up our relationship. She keeps telling me about her loneliness and her sadness. But despite all the loneliness and the sadness, she always manages to make me laugh. She's one of the few who can get me to laugh out loud, not just to smile politely. Out of loneliness, she bought a bird and stuck it in a cage in the center of the house. There are two sticks in the cage, and the bird jumps from perch to perch all day long. It helps Shadia unwind, but still she thinks she'll probably release the bird before it dies of boredom.

When the war broke out, she managed to break the closure on Ramallah and reach Jerusalem. She dismantled her apartment, giving her furniture to her neighbors and her TV, VCR, and washing machine to friends. She says she could cram everything she owns into two bags. Which is good, because it will make it easier for her to pick up and leave next time.

Now she's about to disappear again. If she's quitting her job at the bar, I probably won't see her in the near future. She runs off for long periods of time, and always comes back with stories like "I've made a film about the Nejaidat tribe in Jordan," or "I've written a script for an Austrian film." They always screw her. They don't pay, they don't broadcast what she's done. Something bad always happens to her in the end, and then she runs away.

I'm so jealous of her now, with her bird and her two suitcases. She's a beautiful girl, and there are lots of people who come to the bar just because of her. Black skin with curly hair and delicate features. The Arabs haggle with her over the bill. She gives in to them, anything just so they'll leave. It's the last shift, and she can't stand the sight of them anymore. The lawyer-or-doctor in the suit is the only one left at the bar. He's swaying already, rummaging through his coat pockets looking for his wallet.

I envy Shadia and she envies me: I have a wife and a child, I know where my house is, and I go back there every night. Not like her. Every time she looks for a home, she has to open an atlas. We're stupid farmers, stupid *fellaheen* who won't budge from our land. She can't be like me.

PART FIVE

The Road to Tira

Date of Birth

My father works at city hall. He issues ID cards, passports, birth certificates, marriage licenses, and death certificates. He works out of a small office in the basement, with a small window and a shutter that can't be pulled down. For fourteen years now, my father's been issuing IDs to the people of Tira. In the past, they had to go to the Ministry of Interior in Netanya to renew their ID or apply for a passport, but now they can do it in the village itself.

Father works from eight to four every day. All the workers at city hall have a reputation for being corrupt. People say they just sit around doing nothing and were appointed because they're related to the mayor. My father hated himself for accepting the job, but Grandma and Mother had pushed him. They wanted him to work in the village, not far away, so he'd always be nearby and they could always find him. Getting that job cost Father everything he believed in. Fourteen years earlier he had supported a collaborator who was running for mayor, and his reward was to be allowed to work for the State. People said my father must have been a collaborator too. Otherwise how could he work for the Ministry of Interior after sitting in an Israeli jail on security charges?

People in Tira hated my father. Maybe Grandma's right; maybe they really were jealous of him. My father didn't have any friends except for Bassem, who'd worked in the packing-house with him. Bassem couldn't get out of bed anymore. His years of fruit picking had finished off his back. Every now and then, he'd have another operation, and Father would go visit him in the hospital. Sometimes he'd take the chessboard along, and Bassem would play from the bed.

I don't remember ever seeing Father making friends with people who were considered well-educated—doctors, lawyers, teachers, or engineers. Sometimes I got the impression that he was embarrassed, that he felt inferior, with that job of his behind the broken shutter.

Father had never been so discouraged. He hardly left the house anymore. Soon as he got back from work, he got into bed and turn on the radio on the dresser. Sometimes he'd come into the living room to watch the news, and other times he'd just stay in bed till the following morning. He didn't have much to do at work. Sometimes, weeks would go by and nobody from Tira would need Father's intervention with the Ministry of Interior. Sometimes he got so bored that he'd renew all our IDs and passports, saying they'd expired. Why walk around with old IDs when he could get us new ones within two days, with the signature of the new Minister of Interior?

My father renewed his own ID card every week. Sometimes he considered changing his name. The fact that this was possible appealed to him. He updated the information: Israeli citizen, Arab, married, father of four. Date of birth: 0/0/47, because Grandma couldn't remember exactly when Father had been born. When the Jews came and she went to register him with them, she couldn't give them an exact date. All she knew was that it had been in the prickly pear season. Grandma says there was a war on then, and nobody paid much attention to dates of birth.

Everything changed when my Aunt Camilla from the Nur-Shams refugee camp in Tulkarm was dying, and father visited her in the hospital in Nablus. Her oldest son, Ibrahim, had gotten out of jail when the Palestinians entered the West Bank, and as a token of appreciation for what he had done on behalf of the State, they gave him a position in the Ministry of Interior in Tulkarm. Granted, his salary wasn't as high as my father's, but at least he had some status. In the hospital, he walked around with a pistol, and the doctors treated him with respect. Thanks to him, they let my aunt die in the fanciest room in the hospital, with partitions between the beds.

I'd stayed at her place when I was little. At night, there were big fireworks that lit up all the houses, and Aunt Camilla explained that they were army fireworks. I thought then that the camp looked so beautiful, with water running through little grooves in the middle of the street, and no sand at all. The children used the English term *ice cream* instead of the Hebrew *glida*, and when they played soccer, they said *hands*, not *yad*. Even then I knew her son Ibrahim was a hero, though I'd never actually seen him.

After my aunt died, Ibrahim took my father to visit the Palestinian Ministry of Interior in Tulkarm. They were going through some old papers, dating back to the days of the British mandate, when suddenly my father spotted his own name with a precise date of birth: May 14, 1948. My father was delighted to be one year younger. He held a big celebration with all our aunts, and even Bassem was taken out of his bed.

Then my father started tracking down the birth dates of my aunts and all our relatives who'd been born before the war, and all of them started celebrating their birthdays. Aunt Fahten, who was seventy by then, even had some performers at her party. She said it was her way of making up for all the years she couldn't celebrate.

The rumor spread through the village, and people started saying Father wasn't a collaborator after all, because otherwise how could the Palestinians be allowing him go through secret documents? The first one to ask my father to find out his date of birth was the mayor, and my father not only dug up his date of birth but provided him with a birth certificate. The mayor had his first birthday celebration in the soccer field, and in his speech he thanked my father for his help.

After that, Father barely found time to sleep. People who couldn't get to him at work would come to our house asking for help. Knowing that he was doing it as a favor, and that it had nothing to do with his job with the Israeli Ministry of Interior, they started bringing gifts in return. Sheep, watches, ground meat, six-packs of Coke, packets of rice and sugar. Some of them offered money, but Father wouldn't take it. He said the only money he'd accept was to cover the cost of the stamps he had to buy in Tulkarm, and he always gave them a receipt signed by the Palestinian Authority. Ibrahim had no problem producing the stamps and official receipts at the same printing press where he used to print protest posters. Father handed all the money over to Ibrahim and never touched it. He said Ibrahim deserved it; he needed to build a house now, and to find himself a good wife. Poor guy, twenty years he spent in jail, and now he didn't even have a mother.

The news of Father's magic spread from Tira to the nearby villages and later to the Galilee. People came in fancy cars, bringing money and gifts, and asked for birth certificates. My father became famous. He didn't consider it a bother. On the contrary, this new pursuit made him very happy. People started swearing they'd seen my father having dinner with Arafat. Everyone in Tira knew it was Arafat who had asked my father to support the collaborator mayor. And the whole business with the Israeli Ministry of Interior was nothing more than a clever Palestinian ploy. The newspapers began singing his praises, thanking him and saluting him as "the well-known Palestinian hero," "son of the brave *shahid*," and "the man who has liberated land and administered justice." My father didn't react to their show of appreciation. He didn't say a word. Mornings he'd work in the municipality building, afternoons he'd go to Tulkarm, and almost every evening he was guest of honor at someone's first birthday party.

Parents' Day

Y our parents are here," my wife says, waking me from my Friday afternoon nap. I'd forgotten they were coming. My mother had phoned the day before and told my wife they were coming to see us. She feels she's missing out on something, and she's got to see her granddaughter. They're in the living room now. My mother's holding her, making noises and expecting a response from the baby, who is dividing her attention between Mother, the bunch of keys in Father's hand, and my brother, who's whistling in her face. Her suspicious stares turn to grunts, and before long she's crying. My mother says it's our fault, that we don't come to visit often enough and the baby doesn't know her own grandparents.

My wife sits the baby on her shoulders and tries to calm her down in preparation for her next round with her grandmother. My wife says my mother doesn't know the first thing about babies, she doesn't show the baby any warmth, and it must be her fault that I'm as screwed up as I am.

I shake hands with my parents. Sometimes we kiss. I don't like it. It feels very strange, very awkward, artificial.

Especially when I kiss my father. I never let my lips touch his cheek, I just turn my head toward his lips, which barely graze my cheek.

"How come you're still sleeping?" my father asks.

"I was working last night."

"At the restaurant?" he asks. He knows it's a bar, but my father is always intent on image building.

"At the *chamara,* the dive," I correct him.

There are big bags of garbage in the living room and an enormous pile of dishes rising out of the sink. Generally my wife cleans up before guests arrive, but yesterday she was home alone with the baby and didn't get to it. She tried to straighten up the living room somehow: to clear away the papers, hand-kerchiefs, banana peels, and peanuts that have been gathering on the table through the week. My wife hates dirt, but she doesn't stand a chance with me. It's all because of me. I never help out with the housework or with the baby. My wife says I'm primitive, and I agree.

My parents ask how we're doing, how things are at work, how the baby is, whether she sleeps through the night or still wakes up every hour. My mother says the baby's thinner, and my father says she's still very fat. He lights up, and I take one of his cigarettes too. Again he says he can't believe I've started smoking. I've been smoking for eight years now, and he still can't believe it. He talks about how bad it is, how much he suffers because of the cigarettes, and how he hates himself for not being able to quit, but when it comes to me, I've only begun and I could still kick the habit, in his opinion. "How much do you smoke?" he asks and answers his own question, "Two or three cigarettes a day?"

My parents hardly ever visit us. Before the baby was born, they never did. Generally they stay about fifteen minutes, and leave. It's been two months since 'id el-fitr, our last visit to Tira, and this time Mother asked Father to make it a longer visit because she misses the baby. All week long she begged him to stay for at least an hour. My father agreed, but under one condition: he wanted Fatma, a friend from his Jerusalem days, to come along. On the way to Jerusalem, he called her and invited her to our house in Beit Safafa, a kind of official meeting place. My mother agreed, as long as she was given a chance to spend as much time as possible with her granddaughter.

Mother detests that Fatma. She won't let anyone even mention her name. Every now and then, Grandma or Father or one of my aunts does, and it always gets on my mother's nerves. She says Fatma's a shameless whore. I've never seen Fatma. All I know is that she screwed up my father's life. Grandma told me once that she'd found a whole bag of letters from Fatma to father—and she burned them all.

The phone rings, and before I have a chance to answer, Father says, "That must be Fatma. Tell her how to get here."

The husky voice of an older woman says my name and notes that I sound like my father. Fatma says she's at the "coiffeur," the hairdresser, and her choice of words leaves no doubt that she belongs to the urban class, the one that uses a lot of European words. She's from Ras el-Amud, but her hairdresser is in Talpiyot, on Ha-Uman Street. She doesn't want detailed directions and makes do with the name of our land-lord. One of the workers at the hairdresser's is from Beit Safafa, and he'll tell her how to get here.

My wife pulls me to the side and says we have nothing in the house. If it was only my parents, maybe it wouldn't matter so much, but there's a guest now too. She says I can't go to the store, because I haven't washed my face or brushed my teeth, and my eyes are swollen. She'll go to the store with my brother. He'll help her carry, too. My brother's a good guy. Never lets you down.

My wife hands the baby to my mother, and the baby starts crying. My mother strokes her, rocks her, walks back and forth with her from the sink to the garbage in the living room, three steps away, trying to calm her down. It's no use. My father lights another cigarette, and I take one too. I don't usually smoke when the baby's around, but since he's smoking anyway, I don't suppose my cigarette is going to make a difference. He smoked when I was little and I'm fine. All my brothers turned out fine.

I open the door. Fatma comes in, wearing a long black dress. She's about my height, my father's height. She has a red scarf over her shoulders. She's dyed her hair and had it blow-dried. She's fifty, maybe more. I don't try to decide whether she's prettier than my mother. They're different. She looks like the society ladies who get interviewed on Jordanian or Egyptian TV. You don't see any wrinkles, but you can still tell her age by the area around her mouth and eyes. Her eyelids are heavy. She blinks slowly as if she can hardly lift them.

She shakes my hand and smiles. She asks if I recognize her, and says that she saw me once when I was very little. My father tells her it wasn't me, it was my older brother. My mother takes one arm off the baby and shakes Fatma's hand, studying her. Fatma is thinner than she is. Fatma asks how she's doing, smiles, and strokes the baby, whose crying grows more insistent. Fatma asks, "What's the matter? What's the matter?" and says I have a beautiful daughter.

Father sits down on the couch, with a cigarette. "You haven't changed," he tells her.

She shakes his hand, sits down, and says that actually she wouldn't have recognized him. His hair's gone white, and he's gained a lot of weight.

Father says, "I haven't gained any weight," and pulls in his stomach as he draws on his cigarette. He goes into the bathroom to find a mirror, then comes back and says, "I haven't gained any weight," and looks at Mother for confirmation.

My wife and brother are back, carrying two bags. My wife looks disappointed. She wanted to get back before Fatma arrived, and now the guest will know that we shopped specially for her. A bottle of Coke is sticking out of the bag, and Fatma says, "Why all the fuss? I don't want anything. I don't drink Coke." She shakes my brother's hand and says he's as good-looking as his father once was.

My wife brings out some glasses and pours Coke for the guests. She arranges some bananas, oranges, and apples in a dish. She pours some peanuts out of a brown paper bag and serves them. She clears away the economy pack of wipes and the breast pump and places the tray near Fatma. "You have an adorable baby. She looks like you," Fatma says, and my wife insists it isn't true.

The couches are all taken by now. Father and Fatma are using two seats, and my brother and wife another two. My mother remains standing with the baby and I pull up a chair and sit opposite Father and Fatma, who are trying not to exchange glances. "Since when have you known each other?" I ask, and exhale some smoke.

Everyone looks at me, as if I've asked a taboo question. In our family, people don't talk. We're experts at concealing details.

"Since when?" Fatma repeats. "I'll tell you since when." My father is still preoccupied with his stomach, pulling it in and running his hand over his shirt, as if trying to make it smoother. "I was a young teacher," Fatma says. "I was teaching in a school in the Et-Tur neighborhood, and after the war in 'sixty-seven they took all the teachers to visit the university. That's where I saw your father. That's how we met."

"And then what? How did you start talking?" I ask again, and my mother says she's not going to vote in the next elections. My father says that he thinks the Arabs owe it to themselves to vote. Fatma doesn't have the right to vote anyhow, because she's not a citizen. But even if she was, she wouldn't take part in elections for the Israeli Knesset. Fatma has stayed thin, she's stayed single, living with her brother and the family. Everyone's in the tourism business. They have a lot of money, a lot of buses. This week, they bought a huge house for one of

their nephews. Fatma likes to buy her clothes abroad, preferably in London. She has money. She's vice principal of a school
in Et-Tur. She clears seven thousand, and she has no use for
the money. Thirty-two years now she's been teaching, two years
more than my mother.

"How exactly did you meet?" I ask again, trying to use
the opportunity to find out about Fatma and her letters.

"I was the best-looking guy at the university," my father
says, and forces a smile, but Mother frowns. Father says he and
Fatma wanted to get married. Fatma cuts him short and says
it's lucky they didn't. "Look how much weight you've gained,"
she says, trying to be a friend of the family. "How do you let
him get away with it?" she asks Mother, and Mother has nothing to say. She feels unwanted and makes do with a nod.

Father says the reason they didn't get married was that he
got stuck. First he spent a few years in jail, and then under house
arrest, and he didn't leave the village. Mother breaks into his
story and reminds herself out loud that she still has some cooking to do. That's it; she doesn't want to stay with the baby any
longer. She's sorry she ever agreed to Father's condition. She
wants to go home. The baby's getting sleepy anyway. Everyone realizes it's time to leave. Fatma says it's Friday and the
stores close early, and she still has to buy a birthday present
for her niece.

The baby's fallen asleep. I'll have another cigarette and
then I'll go back to sleep. I'm on duty at the bar tonight too. I
ask my wife if she's seen my lighter, and she says that because
of me we looked like beggars. It wasn't enough that the house

was filthy because I'm so lazy and primitive, it didn't even occur to me to wash my face and change out of my sweats. She doesn't know where my lighter is, but she thinks Fatma is pretty and knows how to take care of herself. "What's the real story between her and your father?" she asks, and I tell her my father's stolen my lighter.

There's No Beer
in Saudi Arabia

The situation is really pissing me off. I'd like to be an Arab college graduate who works as a garbage collector so I can badmouth the State. But I never did make it through college, and the truth is that my job isn't that bad. I'm not really suffering at work. I'd like to be a dishwasher at some restaurant, to pray in a mosque, to be poor. I'd like the sewage to overflow from the toilet into the kitchen, and I'd like for a donkey to be tied to the fig tree, and for little barefoot kids to be shouting all the time, and for my wife to wear a veil.

Everyone has been turning to religion except my father. Every Ramadan, my grandmother launches a rebellion against the infidels. She tries to force my father to fast, and each time he swears he will, but he doesn't. When we were little, Grandma would count the cigarettes in Father's pack, to see if he'd smoked during the fast. When he didn't fast, she staged a hunger strike in protest, refusing to eat the last meal. Every Ramadan, she tries again, but father refuses to behave himself. She says that when he was little he did wash and pray and go to the mosque every Friday. It's all on account of my mother. Men always follows their wives' example. My mother wants to be pretty; she's afraid if she wears a head scarf she'll look old. She doesn't understand that faith in God makes your face beautiful and smooth.

I think about God a lot lately. It's easy, not like with the Jews. All you need to do to be religious is to wash and pray. You can go on living in the same house, and you don't have to separate from your family. In Moslem families, an Imam and a prostitute can live together in the same house.

I don't remember how to pray anymore. I used to go to the mosque, but that was a long time ago. Our religion teacher would give perfect grades to all students who went to the mosque. I went there to pray until I had my shoes stolen. I searched through the piles for hours, but they weren't there. I started crying and waited for everyone to take their shoes. Finally the only thing left was an ugly pair of plastic thongs. I didn't want to wear those, so I had to walk home barefoot.

Adel has returned to religion. The perestroika got to him. He stopped being a communist and slowly discovered religion. He stayed in Jerusalem when he finished studying. At first he had a Russian girlfriend, but when Gorbachev took over, he left her. He said a Jew remains a Jew. He thought about it and discovered that, if war broke out, he wouldn't want to save his girlfriend. Eventually, he married a Christian girl, because it says that anyone who persuades a single person to join Islam has a sure place in heaven. Adel took on a particularly tough case, a Christian girl from Nazareth, who sported the biggest cross at the university. Her name is Susie, no less. Her parents refused to go along with the idea of her marrying some Moslem *fellah,* so Adel and Susie waited until her father died of a heart attack, and then they got married.

Adel is living a comfortable life. He's a lawyer. He has a new car and three kids. My wife gets along with his wife, so we've become friends again. He doesn't drink anymore and never skips his prayers. Whenever we meet, he tells me how wonderful Islam is. He explains that only prayer will help me cope with my problems, and he prays that God will help me to believe. Adel knows I drink, he knows I don't fast, and yet he and his wife invite us for the last meal before the fast at least twice each Ramadan. Susie converted to Islam. She says she's become convinced that Islam is the right religion and Mohammed is the true Prophet. She prays, she fasts on Ramadan, and the only holidays she celebrates are the Moslem ones. She can't believe she ever sang in a church choir.

Since Adel turned religious, he talks differently and dresses differently. He's much calmer. He keeps saying *el hamdulula.* I envy him. He supports the Islamic movement and its motto, "Islam is the answer." Adel believes that ultimately the Mahdi will come, just as Islam promises, and unite all Moslems. Then the Moslem empire will be the strongest in the world, just the way it was in the days of Omar ibn el-Hatab. Adel says that the more Palestinians Israel kills, the closer the arrival of the Mahdi. The worse the situation, the greater the chances of redemption.

Adel says the Jews and the Americans have advanced technology, but according to the Koran the decisive war will be waged with swords and bare hands. Their sheikh tells them in the mosque that God will inflict a terrible frost on the infidels that will freeze all their planes and weapons. That's why Adel has bought his children plastic swords. He tells them they have to learn to use those swords now. He's stopped taking his children to the doctor and giving them medications, because he says that pretty soon there won't be any antibiotics and the children will have to learn how to overcome diseases without help.

When the war broke out, Adel's Sufi sheikh told his congregation that he'd met the Mahdi at the El Aqsa Mosque. Adel was convinced it was the end. "The Mahdi must be in Mecca by now," he said, "and very soon he will liberate Jerusalem and defeat the Jews and the Americans." Adel said he was going to Mecca to wait for the Mahdi. He wanted to be one of the Mahdi's soldiers and follow him from Mecca, just the way it says in the Koran, because whoever follows the Mahdi has a place in heaven. Adel announced that I was going with him. He had money, and he'd pay my fare. He didn't want to go on his own. He preferred to share his room in Mecca with a friend, not with some stranger, a Moslem who might not know a word of Arabic because he's probably from Afghanistan. Adel signed us both up for the hajj.

There's no beer in Saudi Arabia, not even malt beer. The women are covered from head to toe in black clothes with netting over their eyes. Women are allowed to leave their faces and hands and feet exposed, but they believe that if they take extra precautions and cover everything, their punishment on Judgment Day will be reduced. Adel prays the whole time. Even after the twenty-four-hour ride on the crowded bus, he doesn't pause to rest but hurries to visit the Prophet's grave in Medina. He says that all we have is two weeks, so he has to pray as much as possible.

There's one spot that can only be reached by inching your way forward for hours in a terribly dense crowd, but it's worth it, because the reward for a single prayer there is equivalent to the reward for a million prayers. It's the spot where the Prophet Mohammed used to sit and pray and read the Koran. And anyone who succeeds in reaching it says it feels like the most sublime place of all, the true heaven.

Heaven is divided into compartments, and even the lowest compartment is magnificent: a verdant heaven with rivers of honey and cascades of nectar. Every wish comes true in an instant. Think of a pear—and right away a pear tree will appear in front of you, and the branch will bend on its own and serve the fruit right to your mouth. People in heaven sit on the lawn all day long, like in a park. If you think about women, there they are. Or you can think of both food and women at the same time.

It's hard to tell if the women you get are like the ones in Saudi Arabia. Probably not. The women in heaven are petite and young, and they dress in white. They don't undress, because there's nowhere to undress. Everyone sits on the lawn and watches. In heaven there are no houses, not even tents, because it spoils the environment. In heaven there are no industrial materials. You can think about a Walkman as much as you want, but you won't get it. There are no cars and no planes.

Adel says this is my last chance to return to Islam. He takes me to the grave of the Prophet, and when I say there's nothing inside and that all I saw was a green rug with verses from the Koran on it, he starts crying, and screams at me. For two days he cries, but in the end he decides to let me be. He starts praying on his own, and that's that. In his opinion, I'm a lost cause, and I'm bound to burn in hell.

Hell is divided into compartments too, but even the highest compartment there offers nothing good. You die, and get resurrected a million times a day, and to make sure you suffer, they burn you in fire so intense you can't even imagine it. I'll burn, I'll melt, and then I'll be resurrected and I'll burn again and melt again. There are these gigantic people there who never ever smile. They just stand over you and burn your skin off with a branding iron, the way they do with animals. Anyone who goes to hell hasn't a chance of getting out.

On Judgment Day the entire planet will explode, and a thick cloud will destroy all living things. Then we'll all move somewhere else. Everyone there will stand in line on a thread that's thinner than a single hair. People from every period in history, anyone who ever lived on earth. There will be prehistoric hunters alongside doctors from Hadassah hospital. The deeds of every one of them will be weighed, and any deed can wind up deciding your fate for better or for eternal fire. On Judgment Day, nobody recognizes anybody, not even parents or friends. Everyone's caught up in his own reckoning. Your father will come along and say, "Please, I've been good to you. All I need is one more good deed to get into heaven." And you'll refuse, because who knows? Maybe that'll be the one deed you need to save yourself. Everything you've ever done appears before you, from the day you were born till the day you died. The angel on your right shoulder will report all the bad deeds, and the one on your left shoulder will report the good ones. Or vice versa.

I tried to believe in God, to become part of the big circle of people in white constantly circling the black stone. I tried to become part of the ocean of humanity moving toward the mosques. I recalled how I'd prayed as a little boy. I tried to reconstruct everything they taught us at elementary school. There were moments when I was afraid of being alone in the room, and I started to cry. Adel hardly came back from the mosque at all, and I couldn't stop thinking about my wife and baby. At night, when the streets became a little less crowded, I'd put on the white hat and set out to buy some gifts for the family. The sidewalks were filled with women and small children. Without removing their shoes or clothes, they lay there on pieces of cardboard. Adel put us up at one of the fanciest hotels in Mecca, very close to the Kaba, and from the window of our air-conditioned room, I could see the black stone and the people shoving and crowding to get up close and kiss it. Adel made it. He's large. He dislocated his shoulder but he managed to kiss the stone. "The fragrance of perfume from heaven," he said, before he fell asleep.

Our two weeks there were over. The bus ride back was unbearable. Everyone buys enormous woolen blankets in Saudi Arabia, because they're good and they're inexpensive. The Jordanian guide who held on to all the Israeli passports and counted us each evening told us not to buy more than two blankets each, but some of the women bought as many as ten. Adel and I were the youngest on the bus, and we wound up having to stand the whole way home. We hardly said a word to each other the entire trip. There was a point when Adel wanted to get out right in the middle of the desert, to get away from the Jordanian guide and return to Mecca. He was sure the Mahdi had arrived and was afraid of missing him. "Maybe he's in Jerusalem already," he said when we reached Jordan, but the Israeli soldiers at the border and the clerks who addressed us with overdone politeness assured Adel that the Mahdi hadn't come yet.

Wittgenstein's Nephew

On Independence Day, my wife didn't feel well, and I took her to the hospital. Camouflage efforts that had lasted for years were shattered in an instant. The soldiers at the entrance to the village asked me to stop by the side of the road. Me they're stopping? The youngest Arab ever to learn to pronounce a *p*? I have almost no accent. You can't tell by looking at me. I've got sideburns and Coke-bottle sunglasses. Even the Arabs mistake me for a Jew. I even speak Hebrew with the housekeeping staff. It must be my wife, I think to myself. She's somewhat Arab. Sometimes, when we go to a shopping mall or places like that, I hope people will assume she's Moroccan or Iraqi, and that I'm a western Jew who likes eastern women.

The soldier asks for our papers, and I tell him I used to have a Jewish girlfriend, I studied with Jews, and all my friends are Jews. I know all the Jewish expressions, even army slang. I shut up, and hand him my vehicle license and my driver's license. Cars pass me, some with flags and some without. The people in the cars look like they're sorry for me, and I feel so ridiculous with my sideburns and glasses. On the radio, the military station is blaring Hebrew songs, and I feel like such an idiot for believing I'd done everything to make sure I didn't look suspicious.

I hurry to get past the barricade, turn off the radio, and mutter a few swearwords at the police, at the Jews, at the State, at Tira, and at my wife. I decide I shouldn't be taking it out on her. Poor thing. She must be in pain, and the last thing she needs now is for me to be carrying on. I'll be good.

I ask how she's doing and she says everything's fine.

There are only Arabs in the emergency room. Women who seem older than they are, with head scarves and plastic thongs, drag themselves through the corridors. Sometimes they bite on the edge of their scarves. They seem lost, not knowing where to go. Why the hell do they have to look like that? Why do they even go out of the house? And why are those plastic thongs still being sold anyway?

Just don't let anyone think I'm one of them or that I'm like them. Just don't let them call out my wife's name when it's her turn, or announce it on the PA system. Sometimes, when that happens, I don't get up right away, as if it isn't really my name, or as if it might be my name but they've copied it wrong in reception. So wrong in fact that it took on a new religion and nationality.

My wife doesn't know the first thing about any of that. She doesn't give it a second thought, which surprises and annoys me. She's capable of talking to me in Arabic even inside a crowded elevator or at the entrance to the mall, when we're being processed through the metal detector. She plays with the baby in Arabic in public places. I don't understand why she insists. The baby doesn't understand a word anyway, whether it's in Arabic or in Hebrew.

My wife goes in to be examined and I wait as far away as possible, at the end of the farthest bench. I take out a book in Hebrew that I keep for situations like this, and start reading. It's *Wittgenstein's Nephew*, not just any book. If a doctor happens to pass by, he's bound to be impressed. And I don't open the book at the beginning but toward the end. The last thing I need is for them to get the impression that I just started reading it now. I stare at the book, not only to conceal my identity but also to avoid eye contact with the others. That's all I need now—for some creep to arrive, someone who went to school with me once, in a button-down shirt and clutching his keys, his mobile phone, and his cigarettes all in the same hand. All I need is for him to decide on a sudden display of emotion and kiss me. I look down, and from time to time I cross my legs and turn the pages.

"Excuse me," someone addresses me. She's young, dark-skinned, and fat. Behind her are two more women. They all look the same. Must be sisters. Their religious garb hides some of their ugliness. The woman stresses the words wildly: "She is in a birth condition," she says, and I don't know where to hide.

What should I tell them now? Maybe I should answer in Hebrew. I do that sometimes. Arabs turn to me in Hebrew, and I answer them in Hebrew, because how should I know they're

Arabs? True, you can tell, but if they didn't recognize me, maybe I could pretend not to recognize them either. Then again, with those three, you can't miss it. They're Arabs from head to toe. Maybe I ought to give my "I haven't the faintest idea" shrug? Because I really don't have the faintest idea what they want from me. Why me? Why not someone in a white coat? Is it the book? Did they think I was a doctor on his break?

I lower my voice and whisper to them in Arabic that they should speak with the nurse, and I point toward the nurses' station.

"Ahhh," the younger one says, and shouts out in Hebrew, "Because she is in a birth condition!"

I can feel my face on fire, and I try to conceal it with my book. When my wife comes out, I'll murder her. She's the only reason I find myself in this situation. As if I have the strength to deal it right now. When she comes out I'm going to make such a face that she'll never dare take me to a hospital again.

The Road to Tira

The road to Tira stretches between two rows of cypress trees. They run close together, two tight rows. Then, all of a sudden the cypresses disappear, the fields are divided by a straight horizontal line, and beyond those are the unruly rows of houses, uneven and menacing. Bakeries, restaurants, vegetable stores, garages, spare parts outlets, watchmakers. Everything looks cheap and crowded and empty.

The Jews driving through Tira on their way to Tsur Yigal and Kokhav Yair don't stop to shop anymore. There's a war on. Some of them are scared, and some are getting their own back. So much of Tira was built to cater to them, but they've run away. You don't see them anymore, not even on Saturdays. You don't see their women with the short shorts or the girls with the tube tops. For years they overran the village every Saturday, so you could hardly move. Only the store owners would come out of their homes on weekends. Everyone else stayed out of the way. The older kids would come to the souk to watch the Jewish girls. Sometimes I'd do the rounds myself. The Jews have all disappeared now, with their shouting, their plastic bags, their potbellies, their cars, their keys, their hats, and their sandals. Now, at least, there are no more traffic jams.

We don't need them anymore. The people in Tira have become rich enough. They'll get through this war, they won't starve. They build another floor, and another, and they buy expensive cars, jeeps, and trucks and computers for their kids. They send their kids to extracurricular classes too. Some people even send their kids to Jewish extracurriculars. And one neighbor even built a swimming pool outside his home and bought his younger son a Ferrari convertible. It's all thanks to the Saturday earnings. Some people in the village had only worked Saturdays, and that was enough for them to live like kings. Now it's only the Jewish druggies and pushers who dare come to Tira to shop.

The Hebrew textbooks still speak of the small village. One of the questions goes like this: "What do the people in your village do for a living?" and the right answer is still: "They're farmers."

People continue to get married and to have children. The wife of my older brother—the one who's named Sam for the SAM missiles—is expecting. My younger brother, the one who's two years younger than me, has bought tiles for his bathroom. If everything goes according to plan, he'll finish his shell and get married within a year. There's one shell left.

My parents built three shells, even though there are four of us, because the fourth one is supposed to get their house. But they know that at least one of us won't come back. Now they're worried that the youngest, the one who's six years younger than me, may wind up staying in Tel Aviv. He's studying there, but he also works there all week long, taking care of chronic patients at the hospital. He's broken off with us in Tira. He's let his hair grow long, and he wears earrings. He dresses differently and listens to different music. Sometimes we talk on the phone. The last time we did that, we made a date to meet in Tira. He finally said he'd come to see the baby, but he didn't. He phoned and asked us to give her a big kiss for him, and to put the receiver to her ear so she'd learn to recognize his voice.

This brother and I get along very well. Sometimes I think he must hate me for the things I did to him when I was little. I hope I was little enough. When I get very anxious about it, I call him up and ask him to forgive me and tell him I want to know if he hates me. He always says he loves me more than anything in the world.

I'm six years older, but if he returns to the village before me, he'll get my shell and I'll get my parents' house. Since the house is old, my parents have added a larger piece of land to go with it, to be fair and prevent any problems later on. My father always says, "God help you if you fight among yourselves. That would be the worst thing that could happen." People have been fighting over land for fifty years now: brothers against brothers, cousins against cousins. Some of them lost their lives in the process, and the survivors are still taking revenge. The wealthiest people today are the ones who managed to take over two meters of the souk on Saturdays.

Almost everyone carries a weapon nowadays. My father went to get the muffler fixed once, and they offered to sell him a shotgun for a thousand shekels. He almost bought it, for self-protection.

The neighbors' young son, Ayub, was arrested. I remember him as a shy seven-year-old. My mother says he's an arms dealer. They sent the whole country out to Tira last week. They blocked the roads, they broke into the house, and they pulled up the floor tiles, one by one. My parents knew all along that Ayub was an arms dealer. At first they thought the reason he hadn't been arrested was that he was a civil servant. He had a Uzi, and almost every night he'd shoot a round. "*Brrrrr.*" My mother imitates it. "Automatic." She didn't think he was dumb enough to hide the weapons at home, but that's just what he did. They found a lot. She stood by the fence and watched. Fifty pistols maybe. The police and the soldiers were there the whole day. They combed every corner. They entered our plot too with dogs and metal detectors, but they didn't find anything. The dogs sniffed every flower, because they were after drugs. My mother says the police even climbed up on the roofs of my brothers' homes and searched in my shell too. "Aren't you ever going to finish it?" she asks. "When are you coming back?"

Nelson Mandela

My parents have enormous pink sofas in their living room. I sink into one of them and light a cigarette from the pack my father has left on the table. I move my head back and forth like a sprinkler, trying to disperse the smoke. Our house is ugly. There are electric wires sticking out of the living room wall, and a bell that never rings. Next to it is a clock made of gold-covered plastic, inspired by a lion's mane. Hanging next to the clock is a deer's head, also made of plastic. There used to be two sabers too, but they broke long ago. Three brown wooden plaques hang unattractively on the wall across from me, with the inscription *Allah* in black lettering. On the wall to the left, there's a painting by Ismail Shammout with the inscription *Uda* (Return), and next to that is a picture of a mother and a baby with a flight of ravens hovering over them.

The ugliest tapestry in the living room was woven by my mother. It shows two Japanese women in kimonos sitting near a blue lake with white swans floating in it. She made the Gobelin when she was studying at the teachers seminar in Haifa. She always says she was the first woman to study outside the village, and the fact is she's now the oldest woman teacher in Tira.

When I was at the university, I invited Yossi for a meal at my parents' house. Yossi was my first Jewish friend after boarding school. He marked a new period in my life and proved I didn't have to be stuck with Arabs my whole life. After the meal, he joked about how our sink was in the living room, though the thought of watching the soccer match while shaving appealed to him. When we first met, Yossi said he found it hard to say the word *Arab*, because it sounded like a curse. Later, we became good friends.

Now my father is lying on the big sofa, resting the upper part of his body on two pillows. With one hand he's half scratching and half picking his nose, and with the other he's holding a cigarette. My mother is washing something in the kitchen. My older brother and his wife come in and sit down. She's pregnant, in her fifth month, and they don't know yet if it's a boy or a girl. The brother who's two years younger than me is talking to his fiancée on his mobile. It's a special deal called Family Circle. They bought two mobile phones and they can call each other for free.

Time for the news. My father turns up the volume, moves his hand away from his nose, puts out his cigarette, and lights another. Mother puts a bowl of strawberries on the table and sits down on the carpet at Father's feet. There's no room on the sofa, because Father is taking up three places.

"There are no men in Hebron," my father says. He always provides a running commentary on whatever we're watching on television, analyzing it out loud, to make sure we don't miss anything. Every now and then my mother mutters *Azza, azza*—Oh, no—and sometimes she says *mujrimin,* criminals. My father says if there were any real men in Hebron they'd get their act together and force the settlers out of there. "How many can they kill? Let them kill a hundred thousand. In the end, they'll be out of there. Five lunatics are terrifying a whole city. What spineless nothings they are!"

It's March 30, Land Day, and people turn out to join in a general protest against the expropriations and to commemorate the people who were killed in the 1976 riots. My wife and her parents went to visit their village, Misskeh, where Kfar Warburg is today. They rented a bus and went as a group. They do it every Land Day and every Independence Day. It's like an annual outing. Men, women, and children dress up, take their food and their barbecues, their meat and their alcohol, and head for their village. You can still see what's left of the mosque and the school building. The women gather vine leaves and look for hyssop in the fields, the men play backgammon in the ruins of the mosque, and the younger ones drink beer and smoke joints in what's left of the school.

My father says he doesn't understand why they bother going there. If they really loved their village, they wouldn't have run away in the first place. Those cowards are to blame for everything that's happened. Better to die defending your land. And why did they sell what they owned there? My father refers to the sale of expropriated lands to Jews as *land liquidation.* Anyone who sells has given up. "What kind of men are they?"

In the evening, I join my wife and daughter at her parents' house. They're back from their picnic. My older brother blocks me with his car and comes over to give me the keys. I enjoy driving his car. At least the radio works. True, it's only a short drive, but still it's one of those rare opportunities to listen to music in Tira. I hope it's tuned to the military station, because I'm not very good with these dials. I turn it on and listen. My brother doesn't know how to take care of a car. He can't drive. I've been in the car with him a few times, and it always ended in a fight. I don't have it easy with my older brother.

The radio is playing "*Abu el-Halil*"; I can't believe I'm hearing that song. How could the cassette have survived so long? It's the song we used to listen to in Father's car when we went into the mountains to pick hyssop. I used to know the words, and I discover I still do. I sing along with the tape, as if I've never stopped listening to it. "*Ya Amina, ya abu el-Halil . . .* open the Nablus Gate for us and let us all enter." Then came another song I used to love, about putting the shame behind us and restoring our honor with stones and with blood, about children who are fearless. I laugh, now, at the quality of the recording and the quality of the music.

I lower the volume and drive through Tira. It's Friday, and late, but people are still roaming the streets. Lots of youngsters are in their cars or walking, and I wonder where all of them are heading, and on the night of Land Day, no less. There was supposed to be a general strike, but the stores opened even before noon. People can't afford to lose the income. Besides, strikes scare the Jews who drive through on their way to Tsur Natan and Kokhav Yair. They're good customers.

On the wall in my wife's old room there's a picture of Nelson Mandela, taken long ago, when he was behind bars. The Mandela of those days was young and strong, with a full black beard. Next to him is the drawing of a hammer and sickle, and the red Soviet flag. There are photos of models and beauty queens too, and Egyptian singers like Ihab Taufiq and Amer Diab, and women in bathing suits and dresses dating back to the eighties. The most up-to-date one in the room that my wife shared with her five sisters is of Brandon from *Beverly Hills 90210.* She hung it up there when she was in high school. All the sisters are married by now, and the room with the peeling walls is where we stay on our rare visits to Tira.

My mother-in-law has put the beds together in one of the corners, under the pictures of Ofra Haza and a celebrity model. Ever since the wedding, two years ago, we've had the same sheets waiting for us, the same thick pillows, solid as a rock, and the same scratchy woolen blanket that forces us to sleep fully dressed even on the hottest summer nights. It's very hot in Tira. In the past, people would sleep up on the roof in summertime, but they're too scared now. They don't feel safe anymore. You're not supposed to leave your front door unlocked. The village is infested with thieves and criminals and rapists, especially now that they brought in all kinds of collaborators—and their weapons too.

My wife's old room does this to me every time: Suddenly I'm terribly attracted to her, as if we just met. She always puts on one of her mother's faded robes, and I can't resist. We always make love in her room and continue to hold on to each other in our sleep. In her room, my heart fills with love. She's pretty as ever in my eyes, pretty as she used to be, when we first met. She says these are our best times together, the ones in Tira.

Very soon her parents are going to be renovating the house and tearing down this room. The house has always been in bad shape. Before the first time we went there, my wife cried. I was about to ask her parents for her hand, and she was ashamed to show me where she lived. She kept hoping neither one of us would have to use the bathroom, which is the most shocking part of the house. Her father had knocked ten steel nails into the wall over the sink, for hanging sponges, and wrote the name of each member of the family over one of them. Not sponges you buy but loofahs, the kind you make yourself. Seven of the nails have nothing on them anymore. The only pieces of loofah still hanging there belong to her parents and her youngest brother. He's two years younger than us. He's been plodding away at one of the colleges for the past few years, studying economics, and there's a good chance he'll graduate soon. He has his own room under the house. It used to be a storeroom for oil and olives, and it had an oven too. Then, when he grew older, they put a bed in there, and he moved in. He covered the bare walls with red scarves of the Hapo'el soccer team, and with pictures of the Chicago Bulls, Michael Jackson, Fairuz, and Lenin, and with Land Day posters, like the one of a man sitting under an olive tree holding his blond grandson, who's covered in a *kaffiyeh,* and the inscription WE'RE STAYING PUT.

They're remodeling the top floor for him now, and the parents will get their storeroom back. They don't need more than that, my mother-in-law says, and it's time for their only son to have a home of his own. That way he'll be able to get engaged, be married, and have children.

My Little Brother

My little brother has tied his fate to a different world. He's moved out of the village, like me, but he doesn't mix with the Jews. He doesn't have any friends, either in the village or in Tel Aviv. My little brother doesn't talk. He's always been like that. He can spend entire days without saying a single word. His teachers in the village used to think he didn't understand what was going on in class, because he never took part, never raised his hand in class to give an answer. Sometimes, after parent-teacher day, my father would yell at him, "What are you, a sissy? Why are you so shy?" My brother would hear him out and wouldn't answer. His grades were always fine, so they left him alone.

My little brother doesn't like people, especially strangers. When anyone knocked on the door, he'd head right for his room, even if he was the only one home. And if he happened to come home from school and heard strangers talking inside the house, he'd always wait outside under a tree till the guests left. Anything but meeting people face to face. He was capable of spending hours in the rain or in the heat just to avoid it.

My little brother never answers the phone. That's just how it is. My parents have finally given up on him and stopped telling him off. When the phone rings, he's off to his room. He stays in there with his music—his not-Jewish and not-Arab music.

For some reason, my parents think my little brother loves me. They think we're both kind of strange and different, so sometimes when I'm at home they ask me to try to talk with him, see how he's doing. "Ask him how his studies are going," my mother says sometimes. "Ask him how things are going at the university, if he has any friends, if he needs money, if he manages okay with the food and with his roommates." When you ask him something, he can just keep nodding, and it's hard to tell what he's really thinking. But he mails my parents the transcripts with his grades, so they don't worry, they know he's doing all right.

My little brother is an artist. He draws portraits and still lifes. He doesn't show his paintings to anyone. Sometimes, when I'm at home, I go through his drawers and his notebooks and look at his silent drawings. He wanted to study art, but our parents said it wasn't practical, and that a person needs to have a job first, a profession. Art is a hobby; there's nothing you can do with it. My little brother didn't argue. My parents checked out his grades, decided he was cut out for nursing, and sent him to nursing school.

After that, he hardly ever came home. In the daytime he studies and at night he works. On *'id el-adha*, he took a day off from work and came to the village to see my daughter. It had been nine months since she was born, and he hadn't seen her yet. He smiled at her and tried to pick her up, but he didn't know how. He tried to play with her but gave up because he knew it wouldn't work. He didn't want to play with her in front of everyone. That wasn't his style. He stared at her, and eventually he took her to his room. I have no idea what they did in there. Must have stuck earphones on her head. Anyway, when he brought her back, she was all smiles.

My little brother and I were the only ones in the house who liked to play soccer. I knocked him down once and he broke a front tooth. After that, he stopped going out of the house. He didn't want anyone to see his broken tooth. He stopped going to school and told our parents that he was quitting. He wouldn't even go to the dentist. For almost a full year, he stayed home and didn't see any strangers. It was the tooth that made him stop talking too, because he didn't want to open his mouth.

And since he stayed away from people, he stayed away from barbers too. It's been ten years since then, and his wavy black hair is almost down to his ass. He combs it and ties it in rubber bands. My parents have given up. They don't try to talk him into getting his hair cut anymore, but I'm the only one who tells him it looks nice, because it really does. He likes to look at it in the mirror and to play with it. He takes off his shirt and studies his thin, tall, muscular body, trying to hide it with his hair. His tooth is still broken. That's why he's stopped laughing, though sometimes he smiles with his mouth closed. When he straightens his lips, you can tell he's smiling.

Sometimes I buy him new CDs. I bought him a Discman before he went off to school, because I knew he'd never make it without his music. He straightened his lips and looked very happy.

My little brother has to get back to work now, before the guests arrive, before anyone comes to visit because of the holiday. He's in his room, packing his bag, and I go in with the baby. "She's cute," he says, and I see his broken tooth, which has gone yellow by now. It's been so long since I last saw it. For some reason, I thought it wasn't broken anymore—that he'd grown, that he'd had it fixed—but he had never gone to the dentist. He tried to hide his broken tooth with his hand, pretending to play with his hair, or to scratch the tip of his nose, making a fist and talking into it. The fist makes an echo.

"How are you?" I ask.

"I'm okay."

"How's school?"

"Okay."

"How's work?"

"Okay."

"Do you still paint?" I ask.

He nods. "I paint at work," he says.

My brother works at a hospital in Petah Tikwa, in an internal medicine department. He says he really likes his job, and that it's what keeps him going in life and at school. My brother isn't embarrassed to show me his tooth anymore. He can see I don't stare at it. He knows I listen to him, and I really want to hear what he's saying.

He has a good job. He spends the whole night on a sofa that doubles as a bed, the kind you find in rich people's homes, listening to music and painting. He sits on that comfortable sofa facing the three beds in the last room in Internal Medicine B. His job is to wait for them to die. They don't talk, they don't move, they're hooked up to life support. Sometimes a chest rises, but that's the only movement. Usually they die within a day or two of arriving in my brother's room, but there was one guy who was in a bed for two months before he died.

My brother says you can see when they die. They tremble. He rocks his body, to show me how people die. When someone dies, he calls a doctor, and after the doctor signs the papers, he disconnects the machines and puts a name tag on the person's chest and head. That's all my brother does. Sometimes the nurses go to sleep and ask him not to wake them if anyone dies, and he stays with the dead person until morning. Someone dies on almost every shift. One night, all three of them died, and he became depressed because his shift was over early and he didn't know what to do.

My brother only paints them dead. He turns off the blipping machines and writes it all down before notifying the doctor and the nurses. The people in those beds are old, with awful bedsores. He says the room stinks, but he's gotten used to it. The nurses are supposed to wash them every day, but my little brother says it would be much more dignified not to wash them at all. He saw the male nurses use their feet to turn the patients over when they're being washed. Sometimes, he paints the male nurses. They're disgusting, he says, especially the Arab ones. My brother doesn't talk to them, doesn't even say hello. His only responsibility is to the patients.

My brother has a drawing in his portfolio of a woman who died the day before, but he won't let me see it. He says it's a nice drawing, one he really likes. He calls it *The Rich Woman* because all her teeth were implants.

Egypt

The war has become part of our routine, and I try to put myself to sleep with thoughts of war games. I see myself commanding a whole division, putting everyone in ambush positions and telling them not to move without an order from me. In the morning I wake up and realize I've lost the war again. I've been shot at, and my whole division is dead. The war is with me everywhere, even in my sleep. Sometimes I jump up in the middle of the night and check to see who's shooting at my bedroom and who's shooting at the baby. Sometimes the phone rings and it takes me awhile to realize it isn't a shelling.

Sometimes I think of converting, and sometimes I think I ought to blow myself up or run over some soldiers at the Raanana intersection. I go back to Tira more often, in search of an answer, trying to find out what others like me, people with a blue ID card, have decided to do, trying to see if there's any hope left. I start accepting invitations to the weddings of relatives, visiting new mothers, and paying condolence calls. I've got to go back. Mother says they're liable to load each village onto a different truck, and we'll wind up being taken from Beit

Safafa to Jordan. The people of Tira will be taken to Lebanon.
Mother says we've got to make sure that the whole family is on
the same truck.

Mother says the worst that could happen would be to be
taken to Egypt. Egypt is the worst. They just got back from
Egypt last week. The trip left both of them depressed, especially my father, who's lost faith in the Arab world. He says
they're too busy dealing with hunger and don't have the energy
to deal with Zionism, pan-Arabism, and war. It finally dawns
on him that Nasser is dead and that there isn't going to be
another like him.

My father was stopped for two hours at the border, at
Taba. Mother tells me about it in a whisper because Father
won't talk about it, and she doesn't want him to hear her from
the bedroom. Mother says the soldiers at the border crossing
called up his name on the computer and screamed at him in
the most disgusting way. She's shaking, trying hard to contain
the water that's collecting in her eyes and to keep the tears from
forming. They ordered him to sit on the side. Children screamed
at him, "Shut up!" and took him to another room. Mother says
Father wouldn't have minded so much if it hadn't been for the
other people who saw it happen and felt sorry for him. They
don't understand he's worth more than a thousand of them.
Mother says my father is smarter and worth more than anything in the world.

Ever since the trip to Egypt, my father doesn't want to
fight anymore. He continues to stare at the world news, but
he's stopped providing answers and solutions or offering his

running commentary. He doesn't care anymore about the revolution or equality or land or a free country. My father's given up. He says the Palestinians should give up too, and if he were a Palestinian leader, he'd order them to destroy the El Aqsa Mosque. First, they'd blow it up with dynamite, and then they'd bring in the bulldozers to clear away every vestige of Islam and Arabism. My father says that would be the Palestinian revenge for the silence of Islam and of the Arab world in the face of their suffering. And if the Saudis and the Iranians and the Syrians and the Egyptians and twenty-two Arab states—as the Zionists put it—want the El Aqsa Mosque and Mohammed's El-Quds, let them come and protect it themselves. My father says he's had it, he's fed up; everyone had better just give up like us, like the Israeli Arabs.

My father says the best thing would be for our cousins in Tulkarm, Ramallah, Nablus, and Bakat el-Hatab to receive the same blue ID cards that we have. Let them become seventh-class citizens in the Zionist state. He says it's better than being third-class citizens in an Arab state. My father hates Arabs. He says it's better to be the slave of your enemy than to be the slave of a leader from within your own people.

Nadia (named for Nadia Comaneci), the wife of my older brother, Sam, has given birth to the family's first male grandchild. My father doesn't want the baby to be named for him. He says it would be a bad omen, and the baby doesn't look like him at all. My older brother is searching for a meaningful name. They thought of calling him Beisan (now known as Beith-Shean). And Iz Adin, like the Iz-Adin Al Quassam Brigades. And Che Guevara, and Nelson Mandela, and Castro, and Nasser, and Sabra. They thought of calling him Wattan (homeland), which was what Father wanted to call me originally. They thought of Ard (land) and of Iyaar (May), because my brother Sam had been born on May Day and Mother had received a gift from the maternity hospital.

Eventually they opted for the name my younger brother Mahmoud suggested and called the baby Danny. Mahmoud said the name would save the kid lots of problems. Maybe he'd be laughed at in Tira, but he'd have it much easier at the university and at work and on the bus and in Tel Aviv. Danny was better.

Ever since my wife's parents began the renovations to get the house ready for their son's wedding, my wife and I and the baby sleep on mattresses in Grandma's room. She can hardly see or hear, but she still gets up at dawn every day to pray, sitting down. I always open my eyes when Grandma wakes up. My wife and the baby go on sleeping. I watch Grandma crawling toward the toilets and her shower. I hear her throwing up. I get up quickly and go to her. She's sitting on the floor, trying to reach the toilet bowl with her head, but she doesn't make it. She throws up on herself. "What's the matter, Grandma?" I ask.

"Go back to sleep, *habibi*. It's nothing. It's like this every day."

I hug her and kiss her head, trying not to cry. She hides her eyes now behind her white scarf and says it isn't death that makes her cry. Not at all. She's tired already, and she doesn't want to be a burden to Mother and Father anymore. She says the only reason she's crying is that she used to think she'd be buried in her own land. "Do you remember where the key to the cupboard is?"

And we both cry together.